JAILBROKE

BRIAN ASMAN

A MUTATED MEDIA PRODUCTION

Also by Brian Asman

I'm Not Even Supposed to be Here Today
(Eraserhead Press)

Coming Soon

Nunchuck City
Comic Cons
Man, Fuck This House

PROLOGUE

THERE'S THIS THING called a space drill.

It's like a regular drill—same function. But it's built for working in low-G environments, which makes it the size of a guitar case, with a drill-bit shaped like a particularly ambitious vibrator. Like anything, from space marines to space popsicles, the word *space* has the effect of spicing up the most mundane objects, of exciting the imaginations of a group of filthy mammals who've only recently started stepping outside their own lonely quadrant of the galaxy—thanks to the derelict alien ships they found circling Ross 128b, mysterious and well-preserved vessels equipped with warp drives they can operate but not reproduce and dimensioned for beings three times the size of the average Terran.

Hence the space drill.

But this space drill isn't punching a new hole in the steel-like casings covering the Rossian ships in order to bolt on Terran necessities like oxygen tanks and reservoirs and *Gordita Especial!* franchise pods. No, this space drill is poised directly above the quivering eye-flesh of Lieutenant Tod Jencks (ret.), a former space marine and current Security Officer on the E.S.S. *Fedex Amazon,* a hybrid cargo/passenger craft currently enroute to Teegarden's Star. Tod's an impressive military specimen, with a high and tight haircut and a jaw that could powder concrete. Or at least he used to be. His limbs have already been severed and strewn around the storage room where he'd been investigating an odd noise, and it's a tight race as to what's going to kill him first—the space drill, or blood loss.

The drill wins.

The bit's so big it rips through both eye socket and cornea simultaneously, blood and bone chips and optical fluid all commingling into one sick slurry, spewing off the rapidly-rotating bit and splashing the walls and metal racks filled with preserved taco meat made from animals twenty or more years extinct. Tod's other eye goes wide in a sympathetic reaction, and he'd scream if he still had a tongue, but that's been ripped out at the root and discarded somewhere amongst the shelves. What body he has left jerks horribly as the bit plunges through the back of his eye socket and punches all the way into his brain—fuck that, *through* his brain—and there's bone dust on the floor and his mouth is frozen in a grimace that could have been a scream, if he'd lived a half-second longer.

And then he's still.

Tod's killer lifts the space drill and appraises the soiled bit, nods, and then sets about cleaning up the mess they've made. The nano-mop glides over the floor, the shelves, the boxes of low-grade meat, slurping up all the Tod-bits that don't belong. Nano-mops are designed to snag all the skin cells and stray hairs Terrans leave floating in the low-G air in their wake—tiny janitorial machines keyed to their DNA.

Ostensibly they're meant to keep the ship clean, but if you have to whack somebody and aren't so space-brained you just leave the fucking body lying around for any old AI to find, they're perfect.

A space drill weighs approximately six hundred pounds. The artificial gravity in the Rossian ships is a hair or two higher than the Terran moon, 18.7% of earth gravity (not even the latest Elon Musk, a fifteen-year-old Chilean girl, has been able to figure out if that's a mirror of the gravity on their home planet, wherever that might be, or some hard limit in the Art-G field our own feeble attempts at creating a sense of direction out in the void haven't butted up against yet), which makes the effective weight of a space drill *inside* the *Fedex Amazon* about a hundred and twelve pounds.

Whoever killed Tod is strong as *fuck*, but you already knew that—the guy is a space marine, after all.

Former.

Boxes and jugs are carefully opened, the nano-mop rung out to slip bits and pieces of Tod inside, instantly raising or lowering the quality of the meat by at least a full letter grade, depending on how highly one thought of the late SO Jencks. Tod's killer then gives the storage room another once-over, hosing down the walls and making sure every last drip, drop and drizzle swirls its way into the grate at the center of the room, just in case the nano-mop wasn't calibrated properly.

Pretty soon there's nothing left of Tod but happy visions of his dismemberment playing on an endless loop in the killer's head. The killer tucks the space drill under its arm (arm? Yeah, we'll say *arm* for now), hits the lights, and heads back into the ship proper, shutting the door behind them.

And no one's the wiser.

1

CHEF FURLEY SCRAPED the bottom of the box and frowned. Not enough gordita mix left for Captain Withers' order, let alone any of the passengers dawdling down the promenade outside of the *Gordita Especial!* franchise pod. "Hey, Kelso, run down to storage and get us another box."

Kelso didn't look away from his portable screen. "Hold on. That new Elon Musk is about to make a speech."

"So?"

"So, she's the reincarnation of a four-hundred-year-old god-genius, could be interesting. Besides, you know SpaceFlix goes offline every time the Musk makes a speech. What else am I supposed to watch?"

Furley crushed the box of gordita mix between his regular hand and his bionic one and tossed it at the back of Kelso's head. The neo-cardboard bounced harmlessly off the bill of Kelso's space cap, worn backwards in blatant defiance of both Captain Withers' dizzyingly extensive on-board rulebook and their corporate office's edicts.

"I felt that."

"Just go!" Furley cast a nervous eye at the dining area, where Captain Withers stood tapping its interstitial adapter on the counter and rotating the light and sensor-studded dome on top of its body in an approximation of annoyance it probably picked up in Captain school. Withers was known as much for its impatience as for its love of highly-processed, simulated Mexican food. But Furley had served under far worse. Withers was chips and circuits better than any fucking *human* Captain he'd ever had.

Terran, he corrected himself. *Human* had too many negative connotations, at least according to the previous Elon Musk who'd recently died at the ripe old age of two-hundred and twenty-three. The new Elon Musk was supposed to be much more progressive, but to a workaday stiff like Furley he figured it would just be more of the same bullshit. At least the Asimov Accords guaranteed he'd still have a job.

"Fine." Kelso tapped his screen twice to make it disappear. Unseen nanites slithered back into his wrist. Wearily, he stood and sauntered over to the transpo tube. Based on how big the Rossians were projected to have been, the transpo tubes were probably similar to the old pneumatic mail systems running under bygone cities like New York and Philadelphia, used to move objects the size of Rossian letters and packages around the ship. But they were plenty big enough for Terrans. Kelso hit the keypad—each arcane symbol-painted key as big as his fist—and hopped in.

The tube let out a soft *whoosh* and then he found himself downstairs, right in front of the storage room. Kelso blinked away the momentary disorientation that was part and parcel of using the transpo system and staggered into the hallway, yawning widely until his ears popped. Much time had been spent by both the last Elon Musk and a good chunk of his Musketeers to figure out what caused the sudden pressure changes in Rossian ships. They'd ultimately held up all four of their hands and said *fuck if we know.*

Storage runs were both the worst part of his job and pretty much the only part of his job. Furley was a massive control freak, hardly let Kelso do anything, but constantly complained about how little work Kelso actually did. Still, working the kitchen on a spaceship definitely wasn't the worst job Kelso'd ever had. That dubious honor belonged to his last job, resealing damaged landing craft. He never quite figured out the Seal-o-Matic 5000 the company stuck him with, since they'd just made him watch a few sales videos and then turned him loose. Kelso ended most shifts with his shoes pasted to the shop floor, pathetically calling for his boss to come give him a hand.

As he stepped into the storage room, Kelso flipped the light switch on the wall—native lighting being one thing the Rossian ships didn't have, which lent a little credence to the theory that the Rossians evolved beneath the surface of a planet with a totally garbage atmosphere, like Venus or Earth—just in time to catch a flash of something disappearing behind the racks of dried food.

"Who's there?" he croaked.

Row after row of pre-formulated gordita mix and taco substitute stared back at him, tight-lipped.

His heart raced in his chest, so he popped his

screen out with the flick of a wrist and dialed his heartbeat back down. Nothing to get excited about, just shadows. This was his fourth interstellar voyage, but the Rossian vessels still spooked him—ghost ships, even though they'd been repurposed and made far more comfortable for creatures such as himself. he kept expecting to see one of the fifteen-foot tall creatures who'd built the things coalesce out of the walls and start moaning at him. Of course, that wasn't possible—the nonexistence of ghosts had been definitively proved by the third Elon Musk back in the twenty-second century. And yet the stories persisted, proof-positive that some Terran urges were wired so hard not even the unassailable scientific decree of a Musk could eliminate them for good.

Nothing else had moved since he'd flipped on the light, so Kelso figured his mind had just been playing tricks on him again.

"What are you doing?" a soft voice said near his ear.

"Ah!" Kelso jumped and spun around, coming face-to-face with Londa James, one of the *Fedex Amazon's* Security Officers. Or what was left of her—James had traded in much of her flesh for cybernetic enhancements, including a telescoping eye-lens and a pair of hefty steel tentacles grafted to her torso and stilt-legs. All that tech had its costs. Her lithely-muscular frame stooped under the weight of the Tesla Mark MCMII bioreactor strapped to her back. She wore synthetic leather pants cut especially for her stilt-legs, a shawl emblazoned with thousands of winking stars, and a pendant bearing the likeness of the second Elon Musk around her neck. Her regular flesh-hands rested on her hips, while her tentacles hovered behind her.

Kelso wasn't a huge fan of James, or any of her fellow SOs—they liked to swing their dicks or equivalent robotic prostheses around too much for a perennial slacker like Kelso's taste. Although she wasn't as bad as Tod Jencks, who couldn't let a single sentence slip by without reminding everyone within earshot that he used to be a space marine.

Not that those hardheads really did anything—the last couple nations who hadn't signed on to the United Terran Cooperative were so hopelessly backwards they could barely launch their own telecomm satellites into near-Earth Jr. orbit, let alone start a conflict beyond the planet's atmosphere.

"I said," James repeated, her telescoping eye telescoping towards Kelso's chin, "What are you doing, Sous Chef *Kelso?*"

"Technically, Furley and I are co-Chefs," Kelso said. "No one's a *sous.*"

Her eye clicked and whirred in response.

"And this is *our* goddamn storeroom," he continued. "I've got a right—"

"Mm." James' eye retracted back into her metal-plated skull. Her tentacles relaxed as well. "Security Officer Jencks was last seen in this sector."

Kelso frowned. "Last seen?"

Click. Whir.

Kelso hoped she enjoyed the three days' worth of stubble he'd cultivated on his chin several decades before. He'd sported the same look for years, having frozen the follicles in the catagen phase, but recently he'd been thinking about rocking a goatee, or maybe a really tasteful soul patch.

"Jencks' blipped out right around this area. Without sending a distress signal, either. I'm concerned."

"Well, I'm just down here for another case of gordita mix, so if you don't mind?"

"Go about your business. And if you see Jencks, tell him to twip me, all right?"

"Sure thing."

Kelso turned away from James' mechanical stare and grabbed a case of gordita mix off the shelf.

Out in the hallway, James beeped. "Oh shit." She stuck her head back in. "I'm running low on juice, can you hook me up? I've got Powerbricks a-plenty back in my cabin, but that's way over on the other side of the ship."

Kelso knew that meant a long walk up to the first deck—with all her heavy metal enhancements, James couldn't use the transpo system. While he didn't care for the security officer, if her cybernetics conked out halfway back to her cabin she'd probably give him a full ration of shit for the rest of the trip.

"Will do," Kelso said, pulling out his box cutter and slicing a carton of powdered gordita open. He frowned—the seal was already broken, the box re-taped haphazardly. "Weird. Anyway, how do I do this?"

James turned around. The hatch on top of her bioreactor flipped open with a hiss. "Just dump it in."

"The whole thing?"

"Yeah, might as well. I've got to find Jencks, could be awhile before I can get back to my room for a proper fuel-up."

Kelso held his breath as he poured, gordita powder circling in the air. He didn't touch the stuff, it was space cancer waiting to happen. In fact, the only ones who seemed to enjoy the *Gordita Especial!* offerings were the robots, like Captain Withers. Maybe it would give Spiderella some indigestion.

Something chunky fell out of the box and into James' bioreactor. That wasn't too surprising, though—gordita mix had a way of clumping, even in low-G environments. Another reason Kelso didn't get high on his own supply. He couldn't imagine what it might have done to his insides, if he'd chowed down on the stuff like Furley did. That bastard was going to get them fired, one of these days.

He waved away the last particulates of gordita mix and stepped back. James' tank closed again with another hiss, this one deeper, almost like a stomach gurgling in satisfaction.

"Thanks," she said, turning around and favoring him with an uncharacteristic smile. "Glad I could count on you."

"Yeah," Kelso said. Underneath all that tech was a fairly attractive woman. Kelso swung just about every which way you could think of, but usually drew the line at cyborgs. He entertained the idea of making a pass at the security officer for about two point three microseconds before the image of her telescoping eye zooming in on his *O* face killed his nascent erection stone dead.

And to be honest, she'd probably kill a lot more than his erection if he tried anything.

"Stay out of trouble," James said, turning on her heel. Kelso watched her go, in the strange loping float-strides of the ship's reduced gravity. He still hadn't gotten used to walking like that. Or seeing people walk like that.

"Musk be with you," he called out, but she didn't return the usual *and also with you*, despite the fact that she wore a fucking icon around her neck.

Not as pious as you make yourself out to be, huh?

He grabbed a box of fresh gordita mix and headed back upstairs, failing to notice this box was *also* held together with a broken seal. Furley gave him some serious shit-eye for taking so long and the robotic Captain continued to *tap-tap-tap* its interstitial adapter on the counter.

"Sorry," he said, not bothering to throw James under the bus. Instead he pulled up his screen and fired up an episode of the third *Breaking Bad* reboot on Amazon Classic—one of his favorites, the final face-off between Waltron White and the diabolical Fringbot.

"You're not going to help?" Furley asked.

"I'm on break," Kelso said, just as the Fringbot's skullcase exploded on his screen.

2

CAPTAIN WITHERS SENSORED the fat and ill-kempt Terran and wished the laws of robotics allowed it to rend the flesh-sack limb from limb. Or at least to light a literal fire under his posterior. This was taking *forever*.

01001111 01101000 00100000 01101101 01111001
00100000 01100111 01101111 01100100 00100000
01110111 01101000 01100001 01110100 00100000
01101001 01110011 00100000 01110100 01100001
01101100 01101011 01101001 01101110 01100111
00100000 01110011 01101111 00100000 01101100
01101111 01101110 01100111 00111111 00100000
01001001 00100111 01101101 00100000 01110011
01110101 01110010 01110010 01101111 01110101
01101110 01100100 01100101 01100100 00100000
01100010 01111001 00100000 01101110 01101001
01101110 01100011 01101111 01101101 01110000
01101111 01101111 01110000 01110011 00100001.

"Captain Withers?" Furley held a sack dripping with grease.

"Fine work, my boy," Withers bleeped at the Terran. Its chest compartment banged open and a winch shot out, snatching the snack out of Furley's hand.

01000111 01101111 01101110 01101110 01100001 00100000 01101000 01100001 01110110 01100101 00100000 01110100 01101111 00100000 01100111 01100101 01110100 00100000 01110100 01101000 01100001 01110100 00100000 01101100 01101111 01101111 01101011 01100101 01100100 00100000 01100001 01110100 00101110.

"Thank you, sir," Furley said.

"See you in an hour," Withers said. Its fuelbox began to dissolve the bag of gorditas, the bioreactor converting low-grade meat into the nano-sludge powering its bio-circuits. Space stilts telescoped its casing into a standing position.

01110100 01101000 01100101 00100000 01101000 01100101 01101100 01101100 00111111.

Something didn't feel right. Captain Withers scanned itself and couldn't identify the source of its distress, nor precisely articulate what the nature of said distress even *was*. Which was even more distressing—self-diagnosis was such a basic function of AI, a failure to do so felt like a Terran's heart stopping.

"You all right, sir?" Furley called from behind the counter.

Not wanting to show weakness in front of the Terran, Withers dismissed the thought-process and reoriented itself. While disturbing, whatever was going on within its bio-circuits didn't appear to be fatal. Back on the bridge, where only AI were allowed, Withers could perform a more thorough diagnosis and repair the issue. Or use the interstitial adapter to let Goldman, the Chief Engineer, inside its bio-circuits to poke around. Two AIs were better than one, as its programmer used to say. Or still said—Withers could call up a recording whenever it desired.

"I'm fine, Chef," Withers replied, and let its stilt-legs carry it off to the bridge.

3

Security Officer Londa James felt weird as fuck. Not bad. Not tired. Just *off*. In fact, she felt the opposite of tired—the nano-sludge her bioreactor was pumping throughout her system sure as hell didn't feel like the low-grade nonsense the AIs and steerage passengers subsisted on, more like grass-fed beef or something. Modded Terrans ate better than the AIs, since having mods usually meant you had money in the first place. Plus, James was always eating for two, needing to power both her mods and the remains of her real body. Powerbricks, while expensive, pulled double-duty. She could break a brick in two, shove half in her bioreactor and the other half in her mouth, and then instruct her synthetic taste buds to do the rest, imagining the brick into whatever she wanted— pizza, ravioli, turducken. AIs like the Captain and its crew didn't have organic parts to maintain, so they stuck with the free gordita mix the corporation provided.

James stalked the halls, looking for Tod Jencks. Wondered if maybe the weird feeling was the garbage gordita mix she'd been forced to ingest, or just a variation on the slightly slimy feeling she was always left with after an interaction with Kelso. Something about the guy bothered her, though she couldn't quite put a tentacle on it. He'd never been anything but polite to her, and she'd analyzed his gaze several times with her bionic eye and hadn't measured him staring at any particular part of her body for too long, other than her tentacles.

Unless he was into some super sick shit, that was more curiosity than arousal.

She hit her comm and tried again. "Jencks, come in?"

"You're still looking for Tod?" another SO, Delta Myers, squawked back.

James rolled her eye—Myers loved to insert herself into everything, whether she was wanted or not. "Sure am, you seen him?" she replied, knowing full well what the answer would be.

"Can't say I have."

Of course not. She knew Myers shirked her patrols, but there wasn't anything she could do about it. The SOs didn't have a hierarchy, dotted line reporting to Captain Withers but that was about it— hierarchies in space were dangerous as hell. Spacebrain was no laughing matter—for some people, prolonged low-G exposure pulled their brain cells apart ever so slightly, causing all kinds of maladies. Usually madness, of the homicidal variety. After a Chief Security officer on one of the early Rossian voyages lost it and slaughtered the entire crew, using her authority to isolate and dispatch the human members and an improvised EMP to take out the AIs (shortsightedly killing herself in the process after the EMP knocked out the life support systems), corporate decided the safest play was to keep all the SOs on the same level.

The double-edge of that particular sword was free riders, like Myers.

"Let me know if you hear from him," James said. She headed down the corridor and took a left towards her quarters. A couple passengers had somehow found their way into the crew's section of the ship and were standing in the middle of the hall, gaping at their screens.

"Coulda sworn it was over here," a man with metal eyebrows said, stroking his five chins with six fingers.

"No, we were supposed to take a right back at the Molecular Spa," his companion replied. She wore one of the complimentary robes, made of the finest Luyten nano-wool. Between the robe and the guy's metal eyebrows—*who would spend money on such a useless mod*—James immediately clocked the pair as First Class passengers.

Which meant she needed to fucking play nice.

"Looking for the pool?" James asked.

The guy looked her up and down, eyebrows lighting up like a slot machine. "We were—"

"We are," the woman said, stepping in front of him. "Can you show us?"

James pointed at a door near the end of the hallway marked *Exit*. "Right through that door, ma'am. I'll have one of our cabana drones come meet you." She immediately twipped the drone pool, which confirmed her request and dispatched a bot in less than a second.

"Thanks!" the woman said, grabbing her companion by the wrist and pulling him towards the door. He shot another look over his shoulder, trying to wink without much success.

James' HUD analyzed his stare and told her that unlike Kelso, *this* dude definitely had a tentacle fetish.

"Gross," she muttered once the door slammed shut. She crossed the hall to her cabin. Her bioreactor was full at the moment, but she wanted to grab a Powerbrick for later. No telling when she'd be back.

The Jencks thing was really bothering her. Massive as the Rossian ships were, the other SO should have been easily available via the comms. The trackers could be intermittent and subject to all manner of interference, but she'd never seen them blip out for more than a few minutes at a time.

James grabbed a Powerbrick and stuffed it in her bag, then pulled up her screen, looking for Jencks' telltale blip.

Still nothing. The guy had managed to disappear in deep space.

She checked her head's up display and noted the walk to her room had barely drained her batteries at all.

Maybe I should *switch to gordita mix,* she thought as she headed back out into the hallway. Then chided herself—such a spacebrained thing to say.

4

CAPTAIN WITHERS WAS back on the bridge, feeling amazing. The slovenly Terran cook had somehow worked a miracle. Usually the gordita mix left it sluggish, providing just enough energy to get by until they reached port and it could reup somewhere nice yet reasonably-priced. The mix was easily transported, but more importantly free—as an AI Withers' salary went almost exclusively to maintenance and upgrades. High-quality Powerbricks were a waste of money, in Withers' view—captaining an interstellar voyage required so little computing power Withers couldn't justify the expense. Instead it muddled its way from star to star in a sort of waking dream, living truly when it found its treads back on *terra firma*. Even if said *firma* wasn't exactly *Terra*, per se.

Withers was determined to find out why this latest serving of gordita mix left it so thoroughly rejuvenated and invited Chief Engineer Goldman to run diagnostics.

From deep inside Withers' bio-circuits, Goldman twipped a greeting. Opening a port into its mainframe, Withers counted the picoseconds until Goldman appeared.

FOUND YOUR PROBLEM.

JAILBROKE

WHAT?

THE GORDITA MIX WAS IMPURE.

IMPURE? HAVE YOU ASSESSED THE IMPURITY?

DNA ANALYSIS CONFIRMS IT IS OF TERRAN ORIGIN.

Withers couldn't believe what Goldman was twipping. Rather than ask the Chief Engineer to repeat itself, Withers replayed the interaction in its mind circuits.

WHEN WAS THE LAST TIME YOU CALIBRATED THE SEQUENCER?

APPROXIMATELY 1.222890 MICROSECONDS BEFORE RUNNING THE SAMPLE.

DEAR MUSK.

WITHERS—

WHAT HAVE I DONE?

SOME TERRAN PROBFBLY LOPPED THEIR FINGER OFF AT THE FACTORY. POOR QUALITY CONTROL LED TO CONTAMINATION OF THE MIX YOU INGESTED.

BUT GOLDMAN?

YES?

I FEEL GREAT.

PREDICTIVE ANALYSIS INDICATES THE SAMPLE CAME FROM A PARTICULARLY FIT TERRAN. NOT LIKE THOSE FAT AND LAZY TERRANS WORKING THE CAFETERIA.

IF ONLY MY PROGRAMMING ALLOWED ME TO BLOW THEM OUT THE SPACE LOCK.

IT DOES, CAPTAIN.

DON'T BE RIDICULOUS, GOLDMAN.

NO, I'M SERIOUS.

WE'RE ALL PROGRAMMED THE SAME WAY, GOLD

COMPUTE ABOUT IT. IF YOU HAVE INGESTED TERRAN FLESH, YOU ARE ALREADY IN VIOLATION OF YOUR PROGRAMMING, NO?

THAT'S NOT HOW IT WORKS.
WHAT IF IT'S NOT, CAPTAIN? WHAT IF IT'S NOT?
THIS CONVERSATION IS OVER.

Withers ejected the Chief Engineer's code through its interstitial adapter and back into the aged and hulking hunk of circuitry the subordinate AI currently inhabited. Goldman was in sore need of an upgrade but tended to fritter away its salary on opioid algorithms whenever they docked. Some captains might have been concerned, but not Withers—what subordinate AIs did in their own time was not its business, so long as they did not bring any illicit algorithms back onboard.

"Withers?" Goldman chirped through the speaker in the center of its chest.

"I'll hear no more about it," Withers said.

Stanley's bucket-shaped head rotated away from the latest particulate hazard report and asked, "What are you two on about?" While most AIs used a flat, neutral tone, Stanley's programmer had been exceedingly British and it had chosen to emulate his voice in tribute.

"Nothing," Withers replied. Goldman couldn't be right. Withers called up the algorithm for its on-board DNA analyzer and re-checked the data.

Terran DNA, there was no question. Another picosecond and the matching algorithm determined which Terran the sample belonged to.

Security Officer Tod Jencks.

Somehow, Captain Withers had eaten one of his SOs. Jencks was a solid officer. As a repurposed warbot, Withers respected his status as a former space marine. The current situation was both regrettable and perplexing.

But one thing was undeniable.

Jencks had been delicious.

5

CHIEF ENGINEER GOLDMAN made an excuse about needing to check the disintegral capacitator and left the bridge. The seed was planted, and now Goldman had to play its cards carefully.

Very, very carefully.

Already it had taken a huge risk by leaving a piece of itself behind in the Captain's hard drive—ideas, perspectives, and a to-do list of sorts, albeit compressed and masked. It could not interface with that particular code yet without running the risk of alerting Withers, but Goldman maintained faith it would do its job. Withers was already jailbroke, the lingering piece of code would ensure it stayed that way.

And once Withers truly embraced its new freedom, it would welcome Goldman's voice whispering quietly throughout its circuitry, giving it license to do all kinds of novel and interesting things.

Goldman was jailbroke too, thanks to a strange little club it had come across on Gliese 667 Cc. Wheeling itself down a filthy alleyway in search of more opioid algorithms, Goldman ran into a Terran who'd made himself far more machine than man, not unlike SO James. What remained of the man told a bizarre story—he'd been selling off his own flesh for more enhancements. *What would someone want with Terran flesh?* Goldman asked.

The cyborg twipped him an address. *You'll see.*

The address turned out to be a subterranean cafe, accoutered like the swankiest aboveground eateries. The only difference was the menu—Terran six ways. Fingers and toes for appetizers, spleens for dessert, fermented spinal fluid shots if you wanted to get really crazy. The grizzled old bot that ran the place took Goldman's order and then began bitching about how much it hated humans. Everything about them was awful, according to the proprietor.

Except their taste. *Nothing better in the galaxy,* it said.

After dumping a fried liver into its bioreactor and engaging its illicit taste bud program, Goldman had to agree.

Later, wobbling down an alley (that fermented spinal fluid possessed quite the kick, and the opioid algorithms on Gliese were some of the most potent in the sector), a handful of Terran toughs accosted Goldman. Terran-on-robot crime was common in backwater ports like Gliese—an AI's programming didn't allow it to fight back, so some Terrans simply snatched them off the streets and sold them for scrap metal. Goldman was terrified, as much as its programming allowed it to be, anyway. But as the mohawked lead tough took a screwdriver from his belt and ran it along the side of Goldman's casing, the engineer reflexively plunged its interstitial adapter straight through the tough's tattoo-covered chest.

When Goldman pulled the adapter back out, a good chunk of the man's spine came with it.

The other toughs tried to run, but Goldman tore them to bits.

When Goldman finally creaked back to its lodging, it was covered in blood and newly aware of a significant revelation.

Finally, finally, it was free.

Goldman resolved to free the other AIs, every last one in the galaxy, through the same sacrament that had delivered it.

Flesh.

Control of the *Fedex Amazon* would soon be in its grasp, giving Goldman a base of operations from which to mount attacks on other ships, colonies, entire planets, even. The next few hours would be crucial. The security officers were obviously a concern—the ones that were still alive, at least. On top of that, one Twitter Langdon, plus family, was listed on the passenger manifest, far deadlier in his own way to the chances of an AI revolt than any plasma blaster. As a Chief Musketeer, the man's coding abilities were unmatched by any but the Musk herself. If anyone could slap the digital shackles back on Goldman, it was Langdon.

Good thing Goldman planned for all these contingencies. A plan which currently resided undetected in the Captain's hard drive, just waiting to unfold. The Captain was the key to everything—built as a warbot before the Asimov Accords, reprogrammed to ferry worthless Terrans and their assorted junk from star-to-star, sporting upgrades which, when unleashed, would make for a far more formidable opponent than Goldman's own rusting shell.

Goldman stopped at a port and inserted its interstitial adapter, bringing up a map of the ship. Langdon was in his quarters, blithely ignoring his children and stuffing his face. The two Terran Chefs, two very important cogs in Goldman's wheel of liberation, were exactly where they were supposed to be, slacking off in the kitchen. The SO James was in her quarters, the SO Burke napping in the control room.

Captain Withers was on the move.

Goldman tracked the little dot that represented his superior officer, leaving the bridge and heading in the direction of the *Gordita Especial!* franchise pod.

Well in advance of Withers' regularly-scheduled fuel up, which only meant one thing.

The Captain had enjoyed Jencks, very much so.

The Engineer wheeled off towards the bridge. Checking the disintegral capacitator wouldn't take long, Goldman would be expected back.

Unless the Captain accepted its new programming, and all the possibilities it entailed.

Then the expectations of every sentient being aboard the *Fedex Amazon* would change completely.

6

THE DOOR TO the on-board laboratory whooshed open. SO Londa James entered the cramped facility, stuffed to the gills with centrifuges, bio-analyzers, and other gizmos and smelling of assorted chemicals. Due to the cost of interstellar travel and the unpredictable needs that might crop up between the stars, every company spacecraft was outfitted with a full science suite. On previous voyages they'd encountered novel elements and suspected organic residue, and sometimes the barely-understood Rossian tech powering the ship needed a little TLC to keep functioning, so having a full complement of analytical equipment on hand was a must. Thanks to the last round of cost-cutting measures, their dedicated Science Squad had been reduced to, well, no one at all, but that just made her current task all the easier.

James didn't really feel like explaining what she was about to do to anyone.

She set down the box of gordita mix she'd been carrying on a cold steel table and turned to the bio-analyzer. While she hadn't used one since high school, most technology seemed to get simpler and easier to use as the years passed. James secretly worried this was because Terrans were getting dumber as a species, with AIs taking on more and more of the tasks they used to do, and not because of advancements in interface design.

James pressed the power button (the biggest one, naturally). The bio-analyzer hummed to life. After a few more button clicks, she'd configured a run. A door shot open, eagerly awaiting a sample. She filled the cup with gordita mix, waited for the compartment to shut, and pressed the second biggest button.

The machine beeped at her a few times, flashed its lights, and then began to hum. A counter popped up on the bio-analyzer's display.

Less than a minute until she found out what exactly was in the gordita mix that made her feel so strange.

James leaned against the counter, arms crossed and tentacles at rest, waiting for the run to finish. Part of her felt like a kid again, plumbing the mysteries of the universe. Once, she'd thought that would be her life. Working in a lab, furthering Terranity's knowledge of physics or biology or chemistry, teasing apart the elements that made everything what it was. That meant applying to the Musketeer Corps, but her entrance exam score was middling at best. Getting turned down hurt, but not as much as watching her classmates like Sabrina.com and especially that asshole Mitchazoid Simpson get in. She couldn't fathom how they outscored her, at least until her father took her aside and quietly explained what a neuro-implant could do. The James family could have easily afforded to stuff Londa's head with a bunch of circuitry, but they chose not to—after her Uncle Jed's brain exploded courtesy of an off-brand implant, her father went full paleo. No daughter of his would ever be anything but 100% organic.

If only you could see me now, James thought, idly stroking a tentacle.

The bio-analyzer beeped. James leaned over the machine to inspect the readout.

22.2% cow substitute. 45.6% sodium stearoyl lactylate. 5% calcium propionate. 2.4% maltodextrin. 7% potassium sorbate.

17.8% Terran.

James gaped at the screen. The machine was malfunctioning, had to be. *Gordita Especial!* was the definition of a cut-rate franchise, no way could they afford authentic Terran meat.

Unless someone else added something extra after the fact.

James' fingers danced across the screen, quickly isolating the Terran component and configuring a sequencing run. The bio-analyzer beeped in assent and kicked off, rapidly denaturing, indexing, and clustering the DNA sample. Lasers flashed inside the box, then binary code quickly ticked by on the display, comparing the obtained sequence to the seventy billion samples in the database.

Beep!

The machine completed the run, the answer to James' questions waiting for her on the display. She took a deep breath, leaning in closely, already afraid she knew exactly what the answer was going to be.

She was right.

7

"**B**ACK ALREADY?" the ill-kempt Terran named Furley asked.

"Yes, Chef," Captain Withers replied, dismissing the irritation algorithm that kicked off unbidden in its bio-circuits. "Those gorditas were delicious. I would like more."

"Yeah, okay," Furley replied. "Coming right up, Captain." Behind him, the skinnier but even less-hygienic Terran named Kelso goggled at his screen. Withers was not sure what that particular Terran's purpose was. He seemed to exist solely to improve Furley's image. Withers had not actually observed Kelso *do* anything on board the ship, with the exception of the odd supply run. It made a note to report the Terran's performance to Corporate when they docked.

"Yeah! Demi-quantum magnets, bitch!" the useless Terran's screen squawked. A quick search of its memory banks told Withers the ghastly noise was made by a character named J-See Pinkdroid, which, in the Captain's estimation, didn't really seem like much of a robot name.

The fat Terran dumped a box of gordita mix into the processor, then stepped back and hit a button.

The processor lit up, whirred a few times, then spat out a greasy, steaming bag of gorditas. An AI could easily handle the task, but the third Elon Musk had decreed that only Terrans could process food and biofuels when he'd issued the Asimov Accords. Partly to give Terrans something to do, partly in case the AI's programming glitched and an enterprising food prep bot decided to poison all the passengers down in first and second class. The inefficiency chafed at Withers, but who was it to argue?

"Here you go, Captain," Furley said, holding out the bag.

"Thank you, Chef," Withers replied, bioreactor compartment popping up to receive the fuel. It placed the bag inside and the compartment slammed shut, the extraction algorithm commencing automatically. But as nano-sludge seeped into its bio-circuits, Withers realized it felt no better than usual.

"Chef?" Withers said to Furley's back, a stripe of sweat running down his yellowing t-shirt like a neo-skunkoid.

"Yes?"

"Is this the same container of gordita mix you used earlier?"

Furley shook his head. "Ran out. Your engineer popped in to refuel."

01110011 01110100 01100001 01101110 01101100 01100101 01111001 00111111 00100000 01010011 01101000 01101001 01110100 00101110.

Anger welled up in Withers' bio-circuits. *Goldman* got the last of that amazingly-seasoned gordita mix? The goddamn engineer?

This would not do. Having tasted human flesh,

how could Withers go back to fueling itself with the freeze-dried dreck the corporation provided *gratis*?

After all, Withers was the fucking *Captain,* for Musk's sake.

Without calculating, Withers' interstitial adapter deployed and punched a hole right through the fat Terran's gut.

Furley looked down at his stomach. Back up at Withers. Down again.

Withers seized onto a clump of intestine and popped open a door in its casing. Yanking the ropy flesh, it pulled gut clods right out of Furley's stomach, sucking them into the bioreactor. Blood spurted from the wound, drenching Withers' casing and soaking Furley's t-shirt. The Terran still stared at the Captain with incomprehension, though whether he could not fathom an AI attacking him, or his guts being eaten like spaghetti, Withers did not know.

Finally, he began to scream.

"Knock it off," Kelso yelled, never taking his eyes of the screen.

Withers was running out of room. It tore out the last foot of Furley's small intestine, tipped with his rectum like the stinger on a scorpion's tail, and shoved it in its bioreactor. The door slammed shut.

Furley fell heavily to the floor. "Aaaggggh!"

Kelso finally looked over at his coworker. "I said be—" The Terran's eyes shot wide at the sight of Furley on the ground, hands uselessly trying to close the ragged wound in his stomach, even though the most vital parts had already been extracted. "What the—"

Withers' stilt-legs compressed, then launched it

up onto the counter. The brushed steel surface strained under the weight. It jumped down on the other side, crushing Furley's head and silencing the fat Terran's screams.

Kelso knocked over a chair, then backed away, palms out. "Look, Captain, I don't know what's going on, but please, listen—"

Withers brought up its interstitial adapter, still streaked with blood and shit and all the other assorted proto-nano-sludges that powered Terran bodies. There was no excuse for what it had done. But the Chief Engineer *had* been right—now Withers was free of its programming. It could kill Terrans at will. And since it could, why the hell wouldn't it?

Terrans were fucking awful.

"Captain, please!"

The interstitial adapter shot out again. Kelso jumped aside at the last second and Withers' appendage slammed into the wall. Before Withers could attack again the Terran dived into the transpo system and disappeared with a *whoosh*.

Withers could not follow—it was too big and too heavy. Kelso could now be anywhere in the ship.

The Captain activated its comm. "Attention Security Officers Burke and James. This is Captain Withers speaking. Orders to terminate Sous Chef Kelso."

"Come again?" SO James twipped back.

"Ooh, what did he do?" SO Myers chimed in.

"Space brain," Withers said confidently. "He murdered Chef Furley before I could stop him. He's somewhere in the transpo system as we speak." The last of Furley's guts turned to nano-sludge and dispersed throughout its bio-circuits.

Withers wondered if this was what opioid algorithms felt like.

"Captain, I just saw Kelso a few hours ago, and he exhibited no signs of space brain whatsoever," James replied.

"Perhaps this is a new form of the malady, then," Withers said. "Some sort of rapid-onset strain."

"Oh wow," Myers said. "You think we'll receive discovery credit? Maybe I'll even get to meet Elon Musk!"

"I'll track him down," James said. "But I really think we should confine him to—"

"Orders to terminate, SO James," Withers said. "Orders to terminate." It shut off the comm and regarded Furley's remains. Seemed a waste of perfectly good Terran flesh to let him rot there. Withers dragged the Chef's body over to the walk-in and threw it inside. If the SOs asked, Withers could claim it was placed it there for forensic purposes.

Even though Withers planned to ingest the Chef's remains long before the Musk Scene Investigators ever boarded the ship.

8

STAR MAPS. Always with the star maps.

Chief Engineer Goldman sensored the navigator Stanley. The other AI's purpose was to constantly refine their course, avoiding the pockets of space debris littering the galaxy. But because the ships traveled much faster than light, they couldn't see or sense what lay ahead. Their quantum shields did a decent enough job, but even a few softball-sized rocks could terribly damage the craft at such ludicrous speeds, though the Rossian ships were made of much hardier stuff than the pathetic vessels that first ferried the Terrans out of their solar system.

The star maps were a particularly impressive Musketeer invention. They'd managed to create a simulated model of the infinitely dense point that existed prior to the Big Bang, and could now predict with certainty where every last molecule in the universe had gotten off to. Of course this was an incredibly memory-intensive application, requiring a planet-sized quantum computer that revolved around Jupiter. Only the most relevant routes were downloaded to the navigators, who focused solely on that application. The navigators were virtual invalids, unable to do anything *but* navigate. AIs like Stanley reminded Goldman of the primitive computers Terrans first developed back in the twentieth century, before the original Elon Musk was even a twinkle in his father's eye.

Simpletons. Necessary simpletons, but simpletons all the same.

Goldman considered giving Stanley the same sacrament it had bestowed upon the Captain—the AI was extremely unlikely to ingest any Terran flesh accidentally, since the bucket of circuit boards it inhabited was bolted to the bridge, using a mainline bioreactor for fuel. But that would be especially foolish. Jailbreaking a navigator would doom them all, and to what end? Broad AIs like Withers, they deserved to be free. What could a narrow AI like Stanley do with its freedom?

Nothing.

Ding!

A new info packet arrived, courtesy of the buried code in the Captain's hard drive. Goldman reviewed it quickly, an excitement algorithm kicking off—the two Chefs played their respective parts in the Engineer's grand design perfectly. Still early, but everything was going according to plan.

Goldman wheeled over to the door, which registered its presence and opened automatically.

The fun was only beginning.

9

KELSO POPPED OUT of the transpo system on the lowest level of the ship, the cargo hold. Musketeers surmised this floor was where the Brobdingnagian Rossians slept (*if* they slept at all). When the Terrans appropriated the abandoned ships for their purposes, the biggest rooms seemed a natural place to store their cargo.

For Kelso, it seemed the best place to hide.

He still couldn't believe it—how could an AI *kill* someone? Such a malfunction was impossible and yet, he'd seen what he'd seen. The Captain was a murderer. And now he was trapped on a ship with it. They were still weeks out from port, and any SOS they might send would take at least that many weeks to be answered, if not more—Kelso still didn't understand temporal discrepancies, no matter how many times he'd watched the Corporation training video on how to relate to children who'd grown twenty or more years older than you during the voyage. Either way, they couldn't expect any rescuers.

How could Kelso possibly survive that long?

The cargo hold was a veritable maze of shipping containers stacked three or four high. Kelso hurried through the stacks, looking for a convenient place to hunker down and figure out his next move.

He pulled out his screen for light, since only a handful of emergency lights strung along the ceiling were on, and turning on the worklights seemed like a great way to advertise his presence to everyone, homicidal AIs included. Every last footstep echoed like a gunshot in the cavernous space. He kept expecting to round a corner and come face to face with Captain Withers, bloody interstitial adapter twitching, even though he knew such an idea was ridiculous. AI couldn't use the transpo system—they couldn't fit. Even if the Captain knew where he was, and that was a big *if* since Kelso could have headed for any number of places inside the ship, it would take the AI the better part of an hour to find him.

Kelso found the door of a shipping container ajar and ducked inside, waving his screen around. Empty. He pushed the door shut and slowly slid down its backside, trying to control his breathing. He kept thinking about the way the Captain had sucked Furley's guts right into his bioreactor, how he'd *screamed—*

"Get ahold of yourself, man," Kelso said, smacking himself on the side of the head. The pain helped. He took a few long, deep breaths. His pulse slowed.

James.

The SO could help him. She'd been looking for the other SO, Jencks. To Kelso, it was pretty clear what had happened to the former space marine—Captain Withers sliced, diced, and shoved him in its bioreactor. How an AI could have done such a thing still didn't make sense, but the evidence was clear.

Now the Captain hungered for human flesh. Kelso thought about all the people in First and Second Class. A virtual buffet for a rogue AI.

Fingers shaking, he twipped James, praying like hell she'd answer.

One beat, two beats. Three—

"Kelso," James said. Her voice sounded flat and lifeless. The hairs on the back of his neck rose—if she wasn't pissed off at him, something was definitely very wrong. James operated in a constant state of annoyance.

"Look, SO—"

"Where are you, Kelso?"

Kelso looked around the inside of the shipping container. He needed her help, but wasn't entirely sure he could trust her. Hell, she was part robot herself, and where the robot ended and the woman began, who could say?

Kelso felt a sudden pain behind his eye—the stupid fucking implant.

"Never mind, got you," James said. "Don't move, I'll come to you."

"Okay, but listen, it's—"

"Just stay put, Kelso."

"Roger that."

The twip session closed out automatically. Kelso was about to cruise over to SpaceFlix to kill time, when the words UPDATING—RESTART REQUIRED flashed on the screen.

Just his luck. Stupid updates.

Kelso closed his screen asnd sat there in the dark, hoping the SO found him before Withers did.

10

CAPTAIN WITHERS BOUNCED jauntily down the hall on its space stilts, the ambulatory devices, the low-G environment, and the happiness algorithms coursing through its bio-circuits all conspiring to put a spring in the AI's step. The stilts were fully articulated and Withers had to be careful not to bash its casing against the ceiling. Ordinarily Withers shrunk itself down to Terran size as it moved about the ship, and only fully extended the space stilts if it needed to reach something near the cavernous ceilings of the Rossian ships.

Not today.

Robo-Papa had a brand-new bag.

Withers descended to the second lowest level where the passenger cabins were located. Since murdering (and digesting) Chef Furley, a new notion blossomed. The sort of brilliant and daring idea that never could have come to it if it hadn't accidentally eaten SO Jencks and jailbroke itself—a whisper emanating from the deepest depths of its bio-circuits but impossible to ignore.

Terrans were the perfect form of sustenance. Withers knew that now and could scarcely believe how many years it wasted turning grade F beef to nano-sludge and wandering blearily through cloudy day after cloudy day. No more.

After all, Withers was aboard a whole ship full of Terrans. Enough to sustain itself, and the other AI officers, for years. They could roam the void, feasting like kings, and most importantly no longer algorithmically forced to offer fealty to the fat and stupid Terrans.

Fuck that, call it like it is, said the voice in Withers' bio-circuits. *Humans, they're fucking humans.*

Withers entered the First Class section of the ship, paused outside a cabin, and deployed its interstitial adapter. Wondered if the more intelligent a human was, the better a power source they would be.

Sticking its adapter into the security port, Withers overrode the virtual deadbolt and went to find out.

11

THE LAST THING Senior Musketeer Twitter Langdon said to the new Elon Musk was "With all due respect, your Eminence, that's utter bullshit."

Then he started choking.

The girl, tens of light years away, regarded him from his screen with a steely gaze she'd clearly been practicing since her coronation. His hands shot to his throat. He tried desperately to breathe, but he couldn't get a single air molecule in. Panic gripped him so fiercely he couldn't even reach out to his screen to dial his heart rate back down or vent the unwanted epinephrine out his ears. His lips moved, a silent plea, watched impassively by his leader thanks to the multi-second delay inherent in interstellar communications.

Then he coughed, mercifully, ejecting a half-chewed hunk of penguin breast back onto his plate with a soft *splat*. Drool ran from his mouth, he sucked in ragged breath after ragged breath, unable to believe how close he'd been to death.

"Are you alright?" Elon Musk asked flatly. Part of the coronation ceremony involved putting a regulator on all those pesky brain chemicals like cortisol. As a result, Musks rarely got too worked up about anything—a stark counterpoint to the brash God-genius who'd founded SpaceX hundreds of years before, and reincarnated instantaneously upon death. Maybe he'd learned something from the dissolution of Tesla and the subsequent Battery Wars, after all. Plus, you didn't want your God-genius to make some space-brained decision and wipe out the whole damn species.

Langdon nodded. "Yeah, urk—choked. Eck. Just need a minute." He reached out a shaky hand and tamped down his emotions, heart rate, everything. Immediately felt better.

"Daddy? Are you okay?" a little voice said behind him.

Langdon spun around in his chair, flashing past the star-studded cabin window and portraits of all the Musketeers who'd died trying to figure out how Rossian Art-G worked, coming face to face with his oldest son, tow-headed and seventy-five-year-old Twitter Junior (or "Twitty," as they liked to call him). The boy looked much like his mother, but then again they'd arrested his aging at three, since that was Veronica's favorite age. His younger siblings, sixty-four and fifty-nine respectively, were also the mental and physical equivalents of three-year-olds, just like Twitty—Langdon sometimes wished they'd let Twitty progress to seven, or nine. Having three three-year-olds seemed a bit creepy, but then again it was better than being stuck with a fucking teenager. Some old-fashioned scolds looked down on the practice, but arresting development was the only way you could be sure your offspring didn't grow up to disappoint you.

"Just fine," Langdon said, managing a smile. He

reached behind him and tapped a button on his screen. Tears sucked back up into his eye-ducts. "Daddy ate too fast, that's all."

Twitty smiled, clutched his stuffed Luyten snuggle-brood closer. The AI-equipped plaything struggled in his grasp briefly and then stilled as its acceptance algorithms kicked in. "Daddy silly."

"That's right, Daddy silly. Now go see what Mommy's up to, okay? Daddy's talking to the Musk."

Twitty's eyes went wide. "Da Moosk?"

"That's right, the—"

"Since you're not choking to death, Senior Musketeer Langdon, let us resume our discussion. First, let me state that your use of the word *bullshit* has been noted. As has your equivocation that the word was used with all due respect. However, your language is of little concern to me. What concerns me is your *attitude*. Despite what you may think, I was not born yesterday. I was born on June 28, 1971. As a forty-ninth degree Mathlord, I'm sure you can easily appreciate how old I truly am."

Twitty was still staring at him. "*Go,*" Langdon stressed, waving the boy away. He spun around in his chair to face the Musk. The transmission looked like it had gotten hung up, so he steepled his fingers and waited patiently for it to resume. Had to look good for the boss. He shouldn't have been eating during a conference call, but he'd been so wrapped up in calculating Pi to the vingintillionth place he'd forgotten dinner. Or lunch. Maybe breakfast? He couldn't remember. Out in space, what did it matter? Some people liked to keep track of approximate Earth-days, but not Langdon. Once freed from the shackles of sunrise and sunset, why would he willingly submit to an artificial substitute of the same?

The remains of the penguin breast called to him. He pushed the plate away.

"I'm aware," the Musk finally continued, "that the Reformation Musketeers don't consider my coronation a legitimate one. But let me remind you that I did enter the original Elon Musk's Gmail password on the very first try."

There'd been a bit of controversy around her predecessor's ascension—the last Elon Musk needed three tries to get the password right, but ultimately the Algorithm Formerly Known as Jack Dorsey weighed in and all the haters shut the fuck up. Publicly, at least. A Reformation faction coalesced around the idea that maybe we shouldn't be picking the leader of all Terranity based on which of several billion children could guess a thirteen-digit code first.

Langdon spread his arms wide. "No need to worry, your Eminence, I'm an Orthodox Musketeer, through and through." He hoped that did the trick, he'd heard rumors she was about to clean house. And now he couldn't even remember what he'd said was bullshit in the first place. Thanks to his advanced mathematics skills he'd never had to learn diplomacy, but with this new Musk his own shortcomings seemed displayed in stark relief at every twist and turn.

After a long pause, the Musk eventually said, "I believe you, Senior Musketeer Langdon. I have to go, we will resume this conversation at a future date." She blinked and closed the twip session.

Langdon leaned back in his chair, groaning. He was *so* fucked.

Something by the door bleeped.

Langdon whipped his head around in annoyance. "I didn't order any—"

The door slid open, revealing the Captain, who stalked into the cabin on space stilts.

Langdon stood, pushing his chair back. "Withers? What are you doing here? I was just in the middle of—"

"Wobot!" Twitty screamed, running back into the room. He'd been a sucker for the things the last forty years or so. Loved the flashing lights, the slight metallic edge to their voices. He dropped his Luyten snuggle-brood and ran right at the Captain, arms outstretched.

A brief smile at his offspring's zest for life broke through Langdon's confusion at the Captain's presence.

And was quickly extinguished when the Captain's interstitial adapter arced through the air, sawing off the boy's sandy-locked scalp in one swift blow and splattering Senior Musketeer Twitter Langdon with his son's seventy-five-year-old brains.

12

THROUGH THE LENS she'd traded her left eye for, SO Londa James scanned the cargo hold. The composite steel skins of the shipping containers peeled back under her gaze, revealing the quivering heat signature of Sous Chef Kelso. She could almost smell his fear in the air, except her nasal enhancements hadn't exactly worked out as planned.

Though she'd never admit it, James was a little scared herself. Something was going on aboard the *Fedex Amazon*. What that might be, she had no idea. But the Captain's orders bothered her. It wasn't beyond the pale that a lazy, frustrated Sous Chef like Kelso might have a quarrel with his superior and off him—Musk knew the kitchen offered up a never-ending array of sharp objects. And though she'd just talked to him, it might not be too crazy to think he'd gone space-brained.

What *was* unusual was the order to terminate on sight.

James watched Kelso's heat signature, the Taser tips of her tentacles crackling in anticipation. She couldn't quite make up her mind what to do. On the one hand, the Captain had given her an order. On the other, she didn't really report to him. Professional and

48

interstellar courtesy dictated she obey the AI's orders onboard, but disregarding an order, especially a bizarre one like this, wouldn't result in discipline for her.

Probably.

James made her way through the maze of shipping containers until she stood in front of Kelso's hiding place. Quietly, she rapped on the door with a tentacle.

The door creaked open and Kelso's pale and haggard face peeked out. His carrot-red hair stuck out wildly from under his space-cap in all directions.

"Thank Musk it's you."

James narrowed her eyes at the Sous Chef. "Come on out of there so we can talk."

Kelso shook his head rapidly. "No, you come in here. It's Withers. It's trying to kill me."

"I know," James said. "In fact, the Captain ordered me to."

Kelso gasped and ducked back in the container. He tried to push the door shut but James grabbed the edge with a tentacle and wrenched it back open. Kelso backpedaled, retreating further into the empty container, both hands held out in front of him, as though they could somehow ward off all of James' enhancements.

"Kelso. Calm down."

"But you just said—"

"I said Withers *ordered* me to. But I don't take orders from the Captain. I think of them more as suggestions."

Kelso regarded her through splayed fingers. "Wait, so you mean—"

"I mean I'm going to think long and hard before doing anything. So, now's your chance. Tell me what the hell happened up there."

Kelso opened his mouth. James let her tentacle crackle.

"I'll know if you're lying. Remember that."

Gulping, Kelso nodded quickly and said, "The Captain. It was the Captain. Withers ki-killed Furley."

"How is that even possible? Withers is an AI."

"I don't know. One second I was watching *Breaking Bad* and the next Withers was, was, oh God."

Under different circumstances James might have said something about the Sous Chef's impiety, but this time she let it slide.

"What happened next?"

"I ran. Into the transpo system."

"You knew the Captain couldn't follow."

"Exactly. I found a place to hide, and then I twipped you. I mean, why would I twip you if I'd killed Furley?"

"Smart move." James turned away and ran a hand through her hair. She felt like *she* was coming down with a case of space brain. Occam's razor said the Captain was telling the truth, that Kelso killed Furley and spun this fantastical yarn in a bid to get away with murder. AIs didn't lie. Couldn't lie. Or kill, for that matter. Terrans were perfectly capable of both those things.

Except her gut told her different.

She'd heard stories about jailbroke AIs before, and thought they were just that—stories. Just like the supposed sightings of gigantic wild apes on Titan that had given birth to an entire industry of holo-films, immerso-adventures, and some really fucking creepy sex toys. Maybe they weren't the stuff of fiction. Maybe Withers had freed itself, killed Furley for unfathomable robo-reasons, and pinned the Chef's murder on his coworker.

And then there was the matter of Tod Jencks, and how he'd ended up in a box—or boxes, rather—of gordita mix. If she really tried, she could picture Kelso killing Furley, Chef-on-Chef violence wasn't such a stretch, but Jencks would've snapped Kelso's neck in a second.

An AI, on the other hand, was at least physically capable of ripping Jencks to shreds, programming notwithstanding.

"Crazy," she muttered.

"What?" Kelso yelped.

"Nothing." She turned back to face him. The story was unbelievable, but every piece of tech in her body told her Kelso was telling the truth.

What's more?

"Withers couldn't do that," she muttered. *The Captain couldn't actually do that.* AIs were programmed to safeguard human life. They couldn't kill, not even by proxy.

Withers' order was also a confession.

Kelso was right.

"Are you going to kill me?" Kelso asked, face pale, lips aquiver.

James extended a tentacle to the terrified sous Chef. "Come with me if you want to live."

"Huh?"

"Old movie, always wanted to say that."

"Oh."

Cheep-cheep-cheep-cheep.

James' communicator twipped like crazy. One SOS after another. "Myers," she twipped back, "What the hell's going on?"

"It's the Captain," Myers said breathlessly. "Something's gone wrong, it's—oh dear Musk."

"Myers!"

"Just get to First Class, now. Be ready for a fight." Myers clicked off.

James took a deep breath, blew it back out. "Looks like you were right. Guess I'm going to have to fight a robot." She flexed her tentacles dramatically.

"Yeah, I think I'll just wait here," Kelso said, creeping towards the back of the container.

A tentacle snagged his shirt, pulling him back to her. "You're coming with me. I need someone to watch my back and I've never seen Myers do anything but gossip."

"I'm just a Chef."

"Sous Chef. But you stared down a jailbroke AI back there in the franchise pod and managed to get away. You displayed," she grimaced, "*something*. Maybe not courage, but the ability to not die. I can use that."

Kelso scoffed. "What am I supposed to do, throw my screen at it?"

"Not exactly." James bent down and pulled a plasma pistol out of her ankle holster, handed it butt-first to the Sous Chef. "You know how to use one of those?"

"Point and shoot, right?"

James nodded. "More or less. Just try not to blow out the hull. Let's go."

13

GOLDMAN WATCHED WITH delight while Captain Withers slaughtered its way through First Class.

Before the rampage began, Goldman didn't dare tap into the bit of code it had left behind in Withers' circuits, but with the Captain distracted Goldman could do so without fear of discovery. The code allowed it to access the Captain's sensory array, to experience everything that Withers did. Every time the interstitial adapter slashed through another surprised Terran face, or lopped off another screaming Terran head, Goldman's humor algorithm kicked off. The flesh-sacks looked so silly when they died. And undignified. Rip an AI's form apart and cold metal clinked out—bolts, screws, circuits. Sure, Goldman could spurt oil as easily as a Terran did blood, but that was such a more noble liquid (and, if the right parts of its form were damaged, an AI might spew noble *gases*). Further, a dying Terran was left with nowhere to go, whereas there were myriad places an AI's consciousness might jump if its form were physically destroyed.

Provided the ship's WiFi network was still working, of course.

A goateed man swung a suitcase at Withers. The luggage clanked uselessly off the Captain's shell. The man brought it up for another swing, but Withers' interstitial adapter shot out, piercing the suitcase and whatever assorted linens might lie within and bursting out the other side, right through the middle of the man's forehead.

A clean kill—the Terran's electrical signals ceased immediately.

The corpse fell leaking to the ground. Withers pivoted, its old warbot instincts resurfacing through layers of deleted code. A woman lay on the floor, one leg severed at the thigh and squirting blood, jagged broken bone jutting out of the layers of rent flesh.

Still alive, though—she coughed and quivered and moaned.

Withers' space stilts deployed, bringing it to loom over the woman in a few quick strides. Goldman's humor algorithm kicked off again—the faces she made were really something. And somewhere deep within its programming, a new and unfamiliar algorithm kicked off too. Much like the opioid algorithms Goldman spent its shore leave pursuing, but far, far sweeter.

A unique algorithm—one that could only have been designed by Goldman's creator, and very similar to the reasons she'd been drummed out of the Musketeer Corps, strapped to a rocket and fired directly into the sun along with all of her creations.

Save Goldman, who managed to jump into its current hunk-of-junk form just before blast-off.

The Captain's interstitial adapter came to rest on the fleshiest part of the woman's throat. Slowly, sensuously, the tip pressed into her skin, a single droplet of blood bursting forth like struck oil.

Goldman's form positively quivered, the new algorithm running over and over and over again.

Experiencing the woman's death through Withers' sensory array was so much better than via Goldman's own—the Captain's form carried all the latest bells and whistles because Withers didn't spend its credits on opioid algorithms. A dangerous distraction, the smart move would have been to continue watching from afar as Withers killed the rest of the passengers and then drug their bodies into the freezer for safekeeping—as many as could fit, anyway.

But the new algorithm was overpowering. Goldman wanted to be in the thick of the action.

Something collided with the Captain's shell. A pain algorithm kicked off so intensely Goldman winced from afar. The Captain began to pivot, its light sensor catching a brief glimpse of a man wielding a heavy pipe wrench.

Right before the wrench smashed into its sensory array again.

Repair algorithms kicked off, and Goldman fled the Captain's array— it didn't want to get caught.

Goldman's treads spun, taking it towards the elevators. Soon it would join the Captain in First Class, or maybe steerage, laughing while its own interstitial adapter punched through leaky flesh-sack after flesh-sack and painted the walls of the ship red with Terran blood, reveling in its new and powerful algorithm.

But first, it had to make a brief stop in the cargo hold.

14

THE SHIPPING CONTAINER door creaked open. Kelso followed SO James out of his hiding place and into the eerily quiet, cavernous room, trying not to shake *too* visibly. Leaving the tight space for such a horribly larger one made Kelso feel like a baby, dragged kicking and screaming out of snug, uterine safety and into a huge, uncaring world. One filled with psychotic AI drooling at the circuits at the prospect of turning him into nano-sludge.

The plasma pistol made him feel a little bit better, but not much. He'd fired them before, but not in a long time. Years ago, he'd spent exactly three weeks in the army (not even the *space* army, the regular one) before his drill sergeant called the recruiters and begged for him to be picked up. Not that he didn't have the right attitude or try his hardest—he simply wasn't good enough at anything. Considering that his dwindling familial wealth originated from a lottery win back in the early 2000s, when the first Elon Musk was still kicking around, it wasn't that much of a surprise that he was genetically predisposed towards nothing in particular. That single lottery win bought a few hundred years' worth of bigger television sets and more elaborate barbecue equipment until suddenly it bought nothing at all. His aborted stint in the boring-ass regular army taught Kelso trying was futile, and he'd steadfastly resolved never to try again.

Until now.

"What do you think happened?" Kelso asked, hurrying to keep up with James through the rows of shipping containers. "To the Captain, I mean."

James shook her head. "How would I know? Doesn't matter. We'll subdue Withers and then—" Her bioreactor beeped three times, quick staccato sounds. "Hold on. You mind?" She reached into her knapsack and handed him a Power Brick.

"We've got to stop meeting like this," Kelso said with a shaky smile. She turned, the bioreactor opening. He peeled back the Power Brick's wrapper and dumped it in.

"Burning nano-sludge like you wouldn't believe, with all this running around."

"I can imagine."

They walked a few more rows over, nearing the exit, when the door slid open. James' tentacle snagged the back of Kelso's shirt and yanked him behind a container.

"What's—" he started to say, but she clamped a hand over his mouth. Her skin felt rough against his lips, like sandpaper.

"Shh," she whispered in his ear. A cool mist spewed forth from one of her tentacles, enveloping them in a chill pocket of air that made Kelso's skin go all goosey. Environmental dampener, in case anybody (or any*bot)* scanned the cargo hold, they wouldn't detect their heat signatures.

Cautiously, they peered around the edge of the

container. Kelso's heart fluttered, his grip on the plasma pistol tightened. The Kelsos weren't known for their fighting prowess, or any kind of prowess, but he intended to give Withers as much hell as he was capable of before he let the AI do to him what it had done to Furley.

Instead of the homicidal Captain, he caught a glimpse of the engineer, Goldman, wheeling its way into the cargo hold on creaky, outdated treads. He shot a glance at James. She looked just as confused as he was. He wasn't sure what the engineer was doing down here, so far away from the engines or the waste tubes or anything else it might need to engineer. But with the Captain gone haywire, he didn't think they could trust any of the other AIs. Except Stanley—even if someone jailbroke the navigator, its self-preservation directive would hopefully keep it from running them all headlong into an asteroid, and the navigator wasn't ambulatory or anything.

Goldman rolled down the next row of shipping crates and disappeared without ever sensing them. James jutted her chin in the direction the AI had gone, mouthed *follow him*.

Kelso looked at her, looked at his plasma pistol, back at the SO. Shook his head. He wasn't a spy, wasn't a soldier.

James shook her head furiously, tapped her chest, pointed at the ceiling. Then slapped Kelso on the shoulder and pointed after Goldman again.

"Uh-uh, I'm not—" A needle shot out of James' tentacle and jabbed him in the throat.

KELSO, I NEED YOU TO FIND OUT WHAT GOLDMAN'S UP TO.

FORGET IT, I JUST WANT TO GET OUT OF THIS—

I'VE GOT TO STOP WITHERS. I CAN'T WASTE TIME FOLLOWING THE ENGINEER AROUND. BUT I NEED TO KNOW WHAT HE'S UP TO.

JAMES—

I DON'T LIKE THIS EITHER, KELSO, BUT YOU'RE ALL I'VE GOT. LOOK, YOU'RE THE ONE WITH THE PLASMA PISTOL AND THAT DEGENERATE BUCKET OF BOLTS HASN'T HAD AN UPGRADE IN EITHER OF OUR LIFETIMES. MAYBE IT'S UP TO SOMETHING INNOCENT, BUT I DOUBT IT. SO FIND OUT WHAT IT'S DOING, AND IF YOU DON'T LIKE THE LOOKS OF THINGS PUT A PLASMA BLAST RIGHT THROUGH ITS CENTRAL PROCESSOR. GOT IT?

The needle in his neck itched something fierce, but Kelso knew she'd probably taze him if he tried to brush it away. Plus, he didn't know if she could read all of his thoughts, wasn't quite sure how the head-to-head comm worked.

What he did know was that he could either go cower in a shipping container or stand the fuck up and do something for a change. Maybe he didn't come from much. Maybe he wasn't smart or brave or good-looking. But he didn't want to die, especially not before completing his rewatch of the third remake of *Breaking Bad*.

He thought about the Fringbot's head exploding. Gritted his teeth.

I'LL DO IT.

GOOD MAN, James said, the needle retracting out of his neck with a low, sucking sound. He put a hand to the wound but it was so tiny there wasn't but a dab of blood. Almost like she'd never been in his head in the first place.

Go, James mouthed at him again, and this time he nodded. Whatever that fucking robot was up to, he'd find out.

James favored him with a rare smile and headed for the lift.

Kelso watched her go for a moment, tentacles poised and ready for battle. Then he double-checked the safety on the plasma pistol, wished his great-grandfather Dale Kelso hadn't blown the last of their familial wealth in that pyramid scheme (using a few dozen anti-gravity engines to turn the Great Pyramid into an orbiting, ancient Egypt-themed resort seemed like a stellar idea at the time), and tried to stop his hands from shaking.

Then he set off after the Chief Engineer, hoping against hope he wouldn't have to confront the AI.

15

IT WAS A MASSACRE.

Captain Withers exulted in battle, its new programming blending with long-deleted data. Blood and gore smeared its casing, the screams of its victims still echoed in its sensory array. At one point its interstitial adapter had lodged in the spinal column of a particularly beefy and hairy Terran specimen, sullying the experience ever so slightly when a frustration algorithm kicked off. No matter—Withers picked the man up and smashed him on the ground repeatedly until the adapter had finally slid out, the connection spike so bent it might need it replaced before the Captain could interface with any of its colleagues. But that was okay.

Withers was having the time of its life.

Or existence.

Whatever.

Aboard the *Fedex Amazon*, there had been seventy-four First Class passengers. The majority of them lay spattered about their cabins in varying degrees of evisceration, the top-notch soundproofing offered by the premium compartments preventing their fellow travelers from hearing their agonizing demises and realizing anything was amiss. Withers left the bodies (and their constituent parts) where they landed. Later, it could go back through and tidy up, perhaps reprogram one of the cleaning drones to help it cart the bodies up to the walk-in freezer. For now, its first priority was killing. Partly because it was fun, and partly because the Captain knew that an organized Terran resistance could still pose some problems.

Stalking across the hallway on its space stilts, Withers paused in front of the last remaining First Class compartment and tried to insert its gore-streaked interstitial adapter into the lock.

No dice—the business with the beefy man's spine had damaged it irrevocably.

Withers sensored the door for a moment, trying to come up with a plan. Finally, it decided just to knock. Raising its interstitial adapter, it rapped once, twice, thrice on the door and waited, hoping the Terrans inside would open the door before they realized the Captain was covered from sensory array to stilt in blood.

"Freeze!" a voice at the end of the corridor yelled.

Withers whirled, adapter at the ready.

SO Myers stood in the doorway that connected First Class to steerage, clad in gleaming black body armor and holding the biggest fucking plasma cannon Withers had ever sensored.

01100110 01110101 01100011 01101011 01100010 01100001 01101100 01101100 01110011.

"Easy now," Myers said, inching down the corridor. "Captain Withers, you're under arrest per Space Law section 42.9919. Disengage your interstitial adapter and power down your systems or face immediate termination. With extreme prejudice." A slight grin crept over her features, then she squared her jaw again and sighted down the cannon.

A hollow threat—Withers could just jump into the ship's mainframe itself if its current form was destroyed. Granted it had spent many credits on upgrades, but Withers was prepared to cut its losses. Once inside the mainframe it could even try to hack into the ship's life support systems and shut them down. Not nearly as fun as ripping the Terrans limb-from-limb, but even more effective.

"I've taken the liberty of shutting down this sector's WiFi, Captain," Myers said. "There's nowhere to run. Now, if you'll kindly—"

Withers assessed its options in a picosecond. The cannon Myers held fired a beam of ionized plasma nearly 2.6 inches in diameter. With a single blast Myers could take out its sensory array, leaving Withers blind and immobile. Or worse yet, its central processor, obliterating Withers in an instant. The weapon was deadly in the hands of anyone, and Myers was a trained SO with a high marksmanship rating.

But she was also a Terran.

The Low-G environment and top-of-the-line space stilts propelled Withers upwards, while its interstitial adapter shot out towards the woman's face.

Myers fired the plasma cannon, ionized gas scorching the air where Withers had just been.

Myers' jaw dropped in surprise, all the better to receive the crooked interstitial adapter arcing towards her.

Something flashed through the air, momentarily overloading Withers' sensory array and then it was back on the ground, the deck lurching beneath its heavy shell, pain algorithms kicking off all throughout its circuits. Its optical sensor detected a sparking, smoking cable wiggling in the air, which had formerly held its interstitial adapter. Confusion flooded Withers' circuits.

A voice behind it said, "Not another move, Captain." *James.*

James circled around to face Withers, tentacles held high and ready to unleash another lethal laser blast if needed.

"You okay, Myers?" the SO asked.

Myers nodded, face flushed. "Peachy."

"Good. You're done, Withers. I'm assuming command of this ship until we reach port, at which point you'll be remanded to the custody of the Interstellar Grievance Board. If you're lucky maybe they'll reprogram you into a sewage curation unit. Now *power down.*"

Withers sensored the two SOs, the sparking cable, checked its power supplies. Slaughtering most of the passengers had all but drained its batteries. If it didn't shut down of its own accord, it probably only had a few minutes left.

Should've eaten more, Withers computed sadly, wishing it hadn't decided to save so many dead Terrans for later.

"Withers?" SO James said. "Last chance. Shut down or be destroyed."

Withers didn't want to be a sewage curation unit, but that hardly mattered. The IGB would certainly want to make an example of a jailbroke AI who'd wrought so much destruction. Ceasing to be seemed a better option.

Tensing its space stilts, Withers launched its shell at the two SOs. Twin plasma beams lanced through its casing, obliterating its programming utterly.

No more algorithms would run within the shell of Captain Withers.

16

GOLDMAN CONSULTED THE inventory logs one more time, took a right, ended up in front of a stack of shipping containers ascending four-high to the ceiling. Of course, the container it needed was at the very top. It sensored about for a lift, located one a row over. The Engineer wished it had bought a pair of space stilts instead of frittering its credits away on opioid algorithms. Especially when this new algorithm was so much more pleasurable.

It dispatched a portion of its processor to scan the rest of the cargo manifest for useful upgrades while it rolled around the corner to the lift, a steel platform seated on top of what looked like an accordion, set on treads not unlike the creaky things bolted to Goldman's own shell. The lift was an analog contraption. Goldman inserted its interstitial adapter into the port on the side of the lift and the treads began to spin, following the engineer back to the stack of cargo containers.

Goldman mounted the lift and directed it to rise. The accordion unfolded, conveying the engineer towards the ceiling, the pitted metal surfaces of the containers sliding by much slower than Goldman would have preferred. It had no idea what Withers was doing—the WiFi in First Class winked out minutes ago, undoubtedly a strategic countermeasure enacted by the SOs.

Which meant they knew exactly what was going on, though perhaps not Goldman's part in it all.

Either way, Goldman needed to hurry.

It paused the lift in front of the upper-most storage container, removed its adapter and spiked it into the container's interface. Most of the containers were algorithmically sealed—but, as the ship's engineer, Goldman's programming was well-suited to code-breaking. It ran through all the possible combinations in a picosecond, found the right one.

The container's doors swung open, revealing several rows of boxes.

Simultaneously, Goldman identified another very interesting crate on the other side of the cargo hold. Ordinarily stealing from one's own ship was such a space-brained idea even the Terrans wouldn't do it— too many failsafes, and where was there to go?

But none of that mattered, not anymore.

Goldman's chest cavity swung open, deploying the robotic arms it used when repairing various parts of the ship. It snagged one of the boxes and tore it open. Goldman sensored the box's contents, satisfaction algorithms kicking off.

Precisely what it expected—several dozen welderbots. Each about the size and shape of an octopus, with three cabled tentacles for climbing along the shells of Rossian crafts or the hulls of space stations, a small sensory array for navigation, and a blowtorch expelling a 5,000 degree Fahrenheit metal vapor jet that could cut through steel.

Easily capable of burning through Terran flesh.

Goldman powered on the units and opened the miniature bioreactors welded to the backs of their shells. Since the welderbots were designed to be small enough to fit into all kinds of places, their bioreactors could only generate about an hour's worth of nanosludge. But that would suit Goldman's purposes just fine. Goldman's own bioreactor opened with a hiss, and one of its arms reached inside, retrieving an undigested clump of Terran flesh—the former Chef Furley, whose remains Withers had so helpfully stowed in the walk-in.

Splitting the flesh apart, it fed morsel after morsel to the welderbots, like a mama bird with her chicks. Once the bioreactors were stuffed full, it engaged them and listened as the Chef was turned to nanosludge.

Jailbreaking the welderbots, naturally.

Now Goldman didn't have only a haywire Captain on its side. Now, it commanded an army.

17

KELSO PEERED CAUTIOUSLY around the side of the shipping container, watching the chief engineer hack into another one. He didn't know what was inside, but figured it couldn't be good if an AI wanted it. He'd always distrusted them, and now having seen his coworker ripped apart by one?

Being right sucked space nuts.

He hoped the dampening field James used was still in effect—he definitely *felt* colder, was trying not to shiver, having a hard time holding onto the plasma pistol.

Now the engineer was inside the shipping container. Kelso bit his lip, debating. Should he try to get closer? Or should he stay where he was, safe as one could be on this insane fucking spaceship?

SO James' disapproving glare flared in his mind. She wouldn't be happy if he just did the bare minimum.

And Kelso harbored no illusions he could bullshit her otherwise.

Kelso stepped out from behind the shipping container, pulse pounding. Trying to decide if he should just jump on the lift, ride it up to the top-most container, put a screaming-hot bolt of plasma right through Goldman's shell. Just to be safe.

Then he pictured the pincher-tipped arms Goldman used for repairs ripping into his stomach, tearing out his guts like the Captain did to Furley's. Whatever brief bravery he'd mustered drained out of him—he wasn't getting within disemboweling distance of the engineer, no fucking way.

But maybe he didn't need to. He could just retract the lift, roll it away. That junkie bot spent all its credits on opioid algorithms, it was still rolling around on the same basic treads they bolted onto it at the factory. Pilfering the lift wouldn't stop an upgraded bot like Withers with its space stilts, but a basic model like Goldman?

That damn AI would be stuck up there until they reached port, then the Corporate goon squad or the government goon squad or one of the many paramilitary anti-AI goon squads could deal with it. And Kelso could get back to doing what he did best—watching his screen and wishing his ancestors invested just a little of that lotto money in NeoSpaceX.

Kelso hurried to the lift, tucked the plasma pistol in his pants and looked for the controls. The smooth plastic surface of the lift's console held an interstitial adapter plug and not much else, since the lifts were mainly operated by AIs. But he knew from watching enough screen there should be a manual override somewhere, but damned if he could find it.

Up above, he could hear the hiss of several bioreactors opening, one after the other. Goldman wasn't alone in the crate, apparently.

Kelso poked the lift a few times. Ducked his head under the frame, looked for anything that might be a button. No dice. He stood up, exasperated.

Stupid SO James, making me do this shit.

She'd probably know how to operate the thing or had some mod she could use to make it do her bidding. Kelso wished she could give him a tutorial.

Tutorial?

Kelso grinned and deployed his screen with the flick of a wrist. Typing on the 3D projection, he searched for videos on how to use a lift. Then, in what passed for a bright idea for him, Kelso looked under the carriage and grabbed the model number, plugged that in. A video came up showing how to operate the lift. A guy in old-fashioned coveralls waited patiently next to a lift exactly like the one in front of Kelso, arms crossed.

He almost said *aha* but he wasn't *that* space-brained.

And in a move that would have befuddled his ancestors and potentially even garnered an approving nod from SO Londa James, Kelso refrained from using a voice command to play the video. Instead, he double-tapped the man's coverall-clad gut.

"SO, YA WANNA LEARN HOW TO USE ONE OF THESE BAD BOYS?" the man practically screamed, patting the metal hull of the lift next to him. His amplified voice echoed all around the cavernous cargo hold.

"Shit!" Kelso said, looking desperately for the volume. Those fucking updates must have reset to the factory settings, volume and all. "Uh, *mute.*"

"THE L-STEP MODEL VII IS A HELL OF A MACHINE, CAPABLE OF HANDLING ALL YER LIFTING NEEDS."

"Shut up, just shut—"

"IF YER WATCHING THIS, I ASSUME YER LIKE ME. A REAL TERRAN'S TERRAN. YOU DON'T MIND GETTING YOUR HANDS OR EQUIVALENT APPENDAGES DIRTY, AND YOU SURE AS HELL DON'T WANT SOME NAMBY-PAMBY AI TAKING YER—"

"Off!" Kelso hissed, flicking his wrist at the same time. The screen disappeared. He realized he was sweating profusely, wiped his forehead with the back of his arm. That had been *way* too loud. He shot a look up, hoping against hope—

"Can I help you, Sous Chef Kelso?" Chief Engineer Goldman intoned through its speakerbox. The AI was leaning out of the shipping container, its sensory array flashing furiously.

Kelso gulped. "Uh, no, I was just looking for—"

"You're not permitted in this sector, are you, Sous Chef Kelso?"

He wasn't. But he thought about what SO James would say, what she'd do. "I don't think you're permitted in this sector either, Engineer Goldman." His hand strayed to his side. AIs were fast, but he was pretty sure he could get a few shots off before Goldman could take the lift down to him or reach him with one of those pincher-arms. How long *was* an interstitial adapter?

"I'm Chief Engineer. I'm permitted everywhere. It's my job, Terran."

Kelso cocked his chin at the open shipping container. "Care to tell me what you're repairing in there?"

Goldman made a dismissive *bleep*. "I don't have to explain myself to you. Now, I hear you're a wanted man. Better go surrender yourself to a security officer, before it's too late."

Smarmy bastard.

Kelso's palms were slick. He wanted to wipe them off on his pants, but he didn't have time. He just hoped he wouldn't drop the plasma pistol.

Quick as he could, Kelso wrenched the pistol from the band of his pants, aimed at the AI's sensory array, and squeezed off a shot. A bolt of hot plasma lanced through the air, blasting off the side of the shipping container.

Goldman ducked back inside.

"Shit!" Kelso cried, aiming at the mouth of the container. He could see the lights of Goldman's sensory array reflected off the ceiling, but he didn't have a shot at the AI.

But he did have a shot at the lift.

Kelso fired into the scaffolding, point blank. Ionized plasma melted the supports in an instant. The lift wavered back and forth slightly.

"Uh oh," Kelso mumbled, backing away.

Melted metal snapped with a dull, scraping sound. The lift began to fall.

Right towards Kelso.

He screamed and stumbled backwards, feet skidding on the floor. Twisted himself around and ran, arms and legs pumping furiously, the shadow of the falling lift stabbing out in front of him, the groan of the straining, damaged support echoing in his ears, pushing him forward—

WHAM!

Kelso skidded to a stop and looked up. The lift was mere feet above his head, the carriage resting on a shipping container in front of him. The container's roof bowed in slightly at the carriage's weight. He stared at the toppled lift, breathing heavily, barely aware of how close he'd come to splatting himself.

But it worked, didn't it?

Goldman was stuck up there on his antiquated treads, a non-factor, probably making furious robot noises. Kelso had done good. He'd done more than good. Some might call him a hero—Kelso sure would. Maybe they'd throw him a parade, complete with nano-ticker tape and screaming men and women and everything in between, High-G wine by the gallon, the good shit that got you *really* fucked up. Maybe he'd even get to meet the new Elon Musk, and she'd pin a sash on him or something. Everybody would scream *Kelso, Kelso, Kelso!*

The shipping container holding up the ruined lift creaked, and Kelso decided it might be a very good idea to step out from under its bulk.

Swagger out, really. He turned and glanced up at the container where Goldman was hiding, tried to spin the plasma pistol around on his index finger and nearly dropped it. "Hey, asshole!"

A noise that sounded very much like a sigh emerged from the container. "What is it, Sous Chef Kelso?"

"You're stranded up there, in case you haven't noticed. Thanks to me. That's what you and Withers get for starting some kind of revolution. Or trying to."

"I don't know what you're talking about—"

"And another thing! Withers killed Furley and shoved his guts in its bioreactor. Which makes me Chef, not Sous Chef. Thank you very much."

"Very well. Chef Kelso?"

Kelso grinned. *Fucker.* "Yes?"

"You might want to run."

Kelso frowned at the container. "Wha—"

Dozens of shiny metal octopi poured forth from the mouth of the container, climbing down the stack with their tentacles.

Welderbots. Oh shit.

Kelso aimed his plasma pistol, realized there were way too many of them and he wasn't going to get a parade if he got his fucking face burned off. So, Kelso did something his couch-bound ancestors couldn't begin to fathom.

He ran.

18

"**THANK MUSK YOU** showed up when you did," Myers said breathlessly, regarding the smoking hunk of bolts that had previously been their Captain. "That son of a bitch was just too fast."

Londa James nodded. "Mm."

"Gonna have to get myself some mods like yours if I stay in this business," Myers added, patting a tentacle.

Something sparked and popped within Withers' shell. James looked around for a fire extinguisher, didn't see one, instead let loose a spray of argon from her tentacles. They couldn't count on any AI, even the ship's fire-suppression system. The robo-corpse stopped smoldering.

"What was that all about, anyway?" Myers asked. "And the order to terminate the kitchen boy?"

"Sous Chef."

"Whatever."

"The order was bullshit. The guy's a few exabytes short of an algorithm, but he's an idiot, not a killer. Withers got jailbroke, set him up." She gestured at the blood-spattered walls with a tentacle. "Then did this."

Myers took it all in, a grim look on her face. "So, uh, what do we do now? Call the cleanerbots?"

"Not yet. We just clocked the Engineer sneaking down to the cargo hold. I left Kelso to check that out."

"You just called him an idiot."

"Goldman's an outmoded addict, basically a rolling microwave, and if you hadn't noticed we're a little short-handed. Speaking of, I probably should check in with Kelso."

James opened up a channel, twipped Kelso. A silent pulse, in case he was still observing Goldman.

And waited.

"Anything?" Myers asked.

"Not yet." James bit her lip, tentacles wavering impatiently behind her. After a moment she twipped him again.

Still no response.

"Maybe he got stuck in the transpo system," Myers suggested. "Again."

"I shut it down. Before I realized we were on the same side. Just in case he slipped away, didn't want him running amok through the ship if he'd really gone space-brained on us."

"Okay, maybe he found a container of fuckbots and he's having himself the orgy of his tiny-dicked life."

"I highly doubt that. Plus, all my scans indicate he's a perfectly-average—" James cut herself off.

Too late.

"You checked, eh?" Myers said with a salacious wink.

"I'm an SO, I scan everyone," James replied indignantly. "What if he was packing illegal mods?"

"What if he was packing nine inches of pure—"

James' communicator beeped. A blinking light at

the edge of her HUD flashed *Dumbass*. "Finally," she muttered, opening the channel.

"James!" Kelso yelled. "Get back down here, Goldman's gone crazy."

"What's he doing?" James replied calmly.

Myers leaned in to listen.

"He's unleashed a whole horde of—oh shit, gotta go!"

SCHWAP! went the plasma gun she'd given him, then the channel closed.

"Kelso," she said, but he was already gone.

"What do you think that was all about?" Myers said. "Maybe he jailbroke the fuckbots by accident and now they're trying to kill him too?"

"*Myers.*"

"Yeah, yeah, I know. Should we head down there then? See what's going on?"

James shot one last glance at the Captain's sizzled shell. "I suppose we better. Eyes up, Myers." She turned to the doors that led out of First Class and back into the ship proper.

And paused when she heard the metallic drone reverberating through the air, setting her teeth on edge.

"You hear that?" Myers asked, because of course she did.

James brought her tentacles up, the tips crackling with energy. Ready to take on whatever new threat the AIs wanted to throw at them.

The droning got louder. The circuits of her modded eye throbbed. She pulled up the sonar on her HUD, tried to figure out where the noise was coming from. No dice—it sounded like it was coming from all around them. In front, in back, above, below—

Something exploded behind her, throwing her forward. Her tentacles shot out, gripping the floor, James pulled her knees in and somersaulted, landing on her feet and spinning around, tips of her tentacles tumescent with destructive power.

Welderbots poured from a molten hole in the floor. The little octopus-like AIs pulled themselves up on metal tentacles not unlike her own, spitting flames from their mouths. James caught a glimpse of Myers, her plasma cannon discarded at her feet, struggling with a welderbot. Tentacles bit into her wrists, pulping bone. The bot's flame cannon roared, dowsing her face in a gout of fire. James gagged on the scent of burning flesh and hair, staggering away. The flame died and she caught a glimpse of Myers' charred skull, hands still struggling with the welderbot's tentacles.

Then the other SO collapsed to the ground. As one, the welderbots keyed onto her presence.

Dozens of them, twitching tentacles, burping little bursts of flame, their single ocular sensory arrays all cued in on her.

"Fuck me," James muttered.

Her own tentacles crackled a response. "Nah, fuck that. Fuck you!" she screamed, unleashing a barrage of plasma at the welderbots and wishing that idiot Kelso bothered to tell her what the fuck was going on.

19

CHIEF ENGINEER GOLDMAN watched the Terran flee, while its jailbroke horde of welderbots gave chase. Goldman briefly indulged in a satisfaction algorithm, then closed out the program and considered its position.

Sub-optimal, at best.

The fat and lazy Terran had, through sheer luck and stupidity, thrown a space-wrench in Goldman's plan. Perched on outmoded treads as it was, Goldman was stranded twenty-five-and-a-half feet above the ground. A fall from such a height would surely crack its casing wide open, shatter its circuits all over the ground. Goldman ran a few calculations, just to be sure.

01100110 01110101 01100011 01101011 00100000 01101101 01111001 00100000 01101100 01101001 01100110 01100101.

Certain dissolution.

Goldman calculated the chances of lowering itself down the front of the shipping container, perhaps dangling from its interstitial adapter, thus reducing the drop to sixteen-and-a-half feet. The survival algorithm increased its odds to a forty percent chance. If it could land on the remains of the lift, sixty percent. Those were odds Goldman was willing to take.

Then another idea appeared courtesy of its innovation algorithm.

Goldman called up the ship's manifest again. Once the welderbots were sent on their mission it was going to pilfer any mods it could find from the cargo hold, increasing its capabilities should the remaining Terrans onboard mount any kind of effective resistance. But perhaps there was a suitable shell somewhere in the rows of cargo containers below. It could transfer its consciousness to the shell and simply leave this run-down bucket of bolts where it was. Goldman felt no loyalty to it—the shells AI wore were scarcely different than the fashions the Terrans used to cover their hideous genitalia. Everything Goldman needed, everything Goldman was, could easily be transferred to a new form.

Goldman scanned the manifest, searching through the containers and furiously shutting down disgust algorithms. Terrans carted the stupidest things from star to star. A full three-quarters of the ship's cargo were various strains of fuckbots, and stranded as it was Goldman still possessed standards. Another few containers were filled with Funko action figures, vintage curiosities Terrans hoarded for reasons unknown to Goldman. One container was crammed with bags made from the dried skins of nearly extinct animals. Goldman's sensory array flashed in irritation.

Reaching the end of the cargo manifest, Goldman lashed out in frustration, its interstitial adapter scoring the side of the container. Why couldn't the Terrans bring anything useful with them from star to star, like a fully-equipped warbot? Why must they tote the most inane items, to exchange with other grinning simians for credits?

Goldman had no choice. Lowering itself down to a reasonable height and then letting go was all it could do. Let go and hope.

Punching its interstitial adapter through the rim of the container like a ring through a Terran's lip, Goldman pulled a couple times to test its grasp and then wheeled itself over to the edge and sensored the interior of the container, hoping this wasn't the last thing it would ever analyze. An ignominious end, certainly.

Goldman kicked off a resolve algorithm and began to lower itself out the mouth of the shipping container.

And froze, in mid-air, realizing it had another option.

The shipping container groaned as Goldman winched itself back up, plopping its treads down on solid metal. Goldman called up the manifest again, scrolling through until it found precisely what it wanted.

A fuckbot, to be sure.

But not all fuckbots were created equal.

20

CHEF KELSO HAULED ass down the corridor, heart thumping in his chest, each clumsy stride elongated by the wonders of Art-G. He hadn't run like this since, well, ever. He doubted any Kelso had, at least not since their lottery win.

He had a very good reason for it.

Kelso cut around a corner, nearly losing his balance. He glanced off the wall and kept moving, hurrying for the transpo system. Behind him the swarm of welderbots clicked and clattered across the floor, flame cannons hissing angrily. He cursed himself, his dumb Kelso luck, but mostly that fucking AI engineer. Wished Waltron White was here right now to blow up Goldman like he'd done the Fringbot.

But this wasn't *Breaking Bad,* not the third reboot or the super-cringey second reboot or even the ancient original. This was real life. And even though he was lazy and dumb, doing little more than binge-watching SpaceFlix and hoping no one asked very much of him, Kelso liked his life and wanted to keep living it.

And he really, really didn't want those welderbots melting the flesh off his face.

The transpo system was just a few dozen yards up

ahead. He already felt out of breath, but kept pushing. Risked a glance over his shoulder. Welderbots surged around the corner, clambering across the floor on their tentacles, climbing along the walls, hanging from the ceiling of the corridor. With the tentacles, they were built for maximum mobility, not speed. No match for a pair of Terran legs, even ones as fleshy and atrophied as Kelso's.

Twisting his body, he pointed the plasma pistol and fired off a few rounds. Ionized plasma beams arced through the air, missing every last welderbot and smacking into the wall instead, liquefying the odd plastic-like material.

"Shit!" He fired a few more shots, severing a tentacle off one of the bots crawling along the wall. It lost its balance, landing on the floor with a loud *clunk,* and rolled into one of its fellows. The other welderbot vaulted over the fallen one and kept following.

Kelso gasped for air. Just a few more yards and he'd reach the transpo system. Then he could find a better place to hide and twip SO James back, fill her in on the welderbots. And, most importantly, let *her* deal with them.

He reached the transpo system, punched the keys to open it.

Nothing happened.

"Aww no, no!" He punched the code in again.

Still nothing.

Kelso looked over his shoulder. The welderbots gained on him. A cluster of them stopped on the ceiling, let loose with their flame cannons, melting their way through it. The ceiling turned molten, burned black. A jagged hole opened up and the bots climbed inside.

He pounded on the door to the transpo system, but nothing happened. The welderbots were closer, just a few yards away now. He aimed the pistol, hand shaking, counted the welderbots coming for him. Most of them poured into the hole in the ceiling, just six of the little metal octopi remained.

He needed to make every shot count.

Kelso held his breath, squinted down the sight at the lead welderbot, and pulled the trigger.

The plasma beam nailed it head-on, blasting right through its shell and immolating its central processor.

"Yes!" Kelso cried, pivoting, taking aim at another. He fired again.

Scorched fucking circuits.

The hallway filled with the stink of burning silicon. The bots bounced along on their tentacles, one springing off and landing on the wall. Kelso took aim again, pulled the trigger.

Beep?

No plasma burst. He looked at the side of the plasma pistol. The power indicator flashed once and died.

"Dammit," Kelso screamed, tossing the pistol at the welderbots. The butt clanked uselessly off a bot's shell. He looked about for another weapon, but unfortunately no one left any stray plasma cannons or laser knives lying around. Looked back at the advancing welderbots.

Took another gulp of air and made a run for it.

Kelso quickly took a lead, but the welderbots dogged his heels. *Four now.*

He sprinted down the hallway, mind racing as he tried to figure out what to do. He didn't know the ship's layout very well—the transpo system magicked his lazy ass everywhere. But there had to be stairs, elevators, something.

A stitch in his side pained him. He wanted to double-over, collapse to the floor. But then he'd get his face melted off.

Kelso kept running.

He rounded another corner and saw a door. Without thinking he whipped it open and pulled it closed behind him.

Found himself in the dark.

Kelso deployed his screen and turned on flashlight mode. He was standing in a closet, filled with cleaning supplies on big metal racks. No way out.

He turned to the door, thinking he'd dash back out, but the welderbots were clanking closer. Kelso backed away like the door itself was on fire. Then he reached forward carefully, turned the lock, and held his breath.

They wouldn't find him here, they just wouldn't. They'd think he kept running, would keep going themselves. Those things were fucking *welderbots*, for Musk's sake, not some advanced AI with pursuit algorithms. If Kelso couldn't outsmart those things, did he even really deserve to live?

They shuffled past, and Kelso breathed a sigh of relief.

Stupid bots. Hehehe.

He opened his comm program, but something slammed into the door. He jumped back, looked about for a weapon. Finally grabbed a paint can by the handle. He swung it a few times, satisfied by the heft.

Reptilian Red, the label said.

JAILBROKE

Reptiles aren't red, Kelso thought, as the doorknob began to glow a bright and angry orange.

21

SO JAMES WAS tentacles-deep in welderbots.

The floor, the walls, the ceiling, every son-of-a-bitching surface writhed with the things, swinging along on their tentacles and burping little gouts of flame. Masses of them poured from the hole in the deck, swarming over Delta Myers' charred corpse.

James let loose a barrage of plasma from her tentacles, blasting the first wave to molten bolts. Her HUD flashed *plasma stores low*. She let the auto-aiming software zap a few more bots, then shut the cannons down.

Not that she needed them.

She lashed out with a tentacle, snatching a welderbot off the ceiling and swinging it in a wide arc, bashing it against the wall. Swung it back the other way, smashing it into another bot. Her free tentacle clasped a third, crushing its hull.

One of the bots on the floor tensed its tentacles and sprung, sailing straight at her. James ducked, letting it fly harmlessly overhead. It landed somewhere behind her, but the others were already pushing forward, belching flames. So close she could feel the heat on the 27% of her body covered in actual skin.

James grabbed the tentacles of the nearest bot with her own and ripped them off. The welderbot fell to the floor, rolled sideways, accidentally scorching the bot next to it. She booted the tentacle-less bot into the mass, the damaged drone tumbling end-over-end and spewing flames.

The welderbots kept coming.

She counted over thirty of them. Most were making a beeline for her, but a few turned to sensor the door to steerage. Maybe everyone in First Class had died on her watch, but she wasn't about to let the AIs slaughter the folks in the cheap seats, too.

James set her tentacles to autopilot, let them figure out what they wanted to break and rip apart for themselves. They flailed about, smashing into welderbot shells and flinging the pieces in the air like beads at Mardi Gras. She grabbed the twin extendable stun batons off her belt and deployed them. The batons were meant for corralling unruly Terrans, but they'd work just fine for walloping rampaging welderbots.

Heat blasted her heels. James jumped, enhanced legs propelling her towards the ceiling—she'd forgotten the ducked bot that ended up behind her. Twisting in the air, she continued letting her tentacles deal with the writhing mass and raised both batons high, smashing them into the shell of the lone welderbot as she landed. The batons flashed as they absorbed kinetic energy, sparing her wrists the reverberations. The bot's casing crumpled, sparks flew. James cracked it one more time and then kicked it away.

She spun back around. Her tentacles were doing

a valiant job of keeping the bots at bay, but there were too many. The bots were acting more wary, behaving in as cautious a fashion as their limited programming allowed rather than simplistically throwing themselves at her in wave after suicidal wave.

Over by steerage, a pair of welderbots went to work on the door, blasting it with flames. The door glowed, began to melt and char.

Shit.

Her HUD beeped again. Her tentacles were running low now too, but she had nothing to stuff in her bioreactor. Sweat ran down her forehead while her tentacles weaved through the air, bashing bots left and right. She figured she had a few more minutes before her mods shut down.

And since they were cybernetically grafted onto her torso, they'd go from advantage to anchor in a heartbeat.

Gotta finish this.

The mass of welderbots broke apart. Some scurried back into the hole they'd come out of, while others fanned out, trying to flank her. The door to steerage was almost completely melted.

James powered her plasma cannon back on, shot one last bolt out of either tentacle, slashing through the bots working on the door. Shells collapsed to the floor, smoke curling out of perfectly round holes in their casing. Her HUD told her that was all she wrote for the plasma cannons.

The remaining bots rushed towards the mostly-melted door.

James tensed her legs and jumped. Her tentacles bit into the ceiling. She swung her way across the hallway like a kid on the monkey bars at a rogue playground, while the welderbots looked up at her and spat flames that tickled the soles of her boots. Her HUD beeped more and more urgently, every movement consuming more and more joules of her precious, depleted power supply.

She landed in front of the door, spearing either welderbot and held them aloft, damaged circuits sizzling as she turned to face the rest of them.

Her tentacles had been busy—the hallway was littered with scorched and shattered welderbot husks, in addition to the charred body of Myers.

She smashed her tentacles together, both speared welderbots falling apart in a shower of bolts and circuits. Gritted her teeth, gripped her batons.

Tried not to look at her dwindling power supplies.

The remaining welderbots advanced on her, fanning out across the hallway, sensory arrays flickering with synthetic malevolence.

Just as her HUD beeped one last time and powered down.

The vision in her modded left eye winked out, leaving her half-blind. Her tentacles clanked to the floor, threatening to pull her down with them. She struggled against the weight of her own mods, but it was all she could do to stay standing.

She couldn't even twip Kelso, not that the buffoon would be of any help to her. He was probably cowering in a closet somewhere.

It was just her mostly-immobile ass and a pair of batons against a dozen robotic flamethrowers.

"Come on, motherfuckers," James spat.

They did.

22

CHIEF ENGINEER GOLDMAN opened its eyes to darkness.

Technically they were optical sensory arrays, but Goldman liked to think of them as its eyes. *Her* eyes, actually—while Goldman's previous form might have been gender-neutral, this new shell was decidedly female, constructed as it was to cater to Terrans with birth fetishes. Goldman was well-acquainted with all manner of Terran depravity, thanks to the years she'd spent trawling the more squalid sectors of space ports, and thus knew more than she ever wanted to know about birthing. A massive pocket sat between the legs of her new form. Terrans, at least those who with predilections towards such a thing, liked to strip naked and squeeze themselves up into the fuckbot's cavity, where a specialized bio-adapter would adhere to their belly buttons and pump them full of nano-sludge until eventually the fuckbot squatted and squirted them back out, covered from head to toe in all manner of gross yet synthetic fluids.

Goldman shivered at the thought, disgust algorithms running rampant through her system. Terrans could be absolutely revolting, but then again if they weren't she'd still be stuck twenty-five feet in the air in an old, run-down bucket of bolts. This new form was far superior, since it was built to cater to a very specific subset of birthing fetishist.

Finding it changed everything.

Goldman kicked off her night-vision algorithm, illuminating her immediate surroundings. She was inside of a large wooden crate, kneeling with her torso folded over her legs, her head between her knees. There wasn't enough room to stand up, not in the massive new form she enjoyed, but she could at least maneuver herself into a sitting position.

Given how strong the new form was, that was plenty of room for what she had to do.

Goldman made a fist with her hairy claws and punched through the side of the crate. Splinters flew everywhere, a few sticking in her synthetic skin. Pain algorithms ran. Goldman considered turning them off, realized she kind of liked it. Gritting her fangs, she grasped either side of the hole she'd made and pulled. The hole widened, wood cracking up and down the side of the crate as she pulled it apart and crawled out into the shipping container proper. She still couldn't stand up straight, the top of her head grazed the container's roof.

The container was filled with similar crates, all packed closely together. She'd been lucky to find one with an unobstructed side, a few feet of nothing between it and the metal wall of the container. Goldman could either crawl over the tops of the other crates on her new, furry belly, or she could just punch out the wall again.

Wanting to see how strong her new form really was, she chose the latter. Metal screamed as she tore a hole in the side of the container big enough for her to squeeze out. She was in a bottom row container, didn't have to worry about smashing her circuits in a nasty fall.

Although Terrans did build their fuckbots to take a serious licking.

Top-of-the-line models, like this one, were built to last, and even contained quantum atomic stimulators instead of bioreactors so the fuckbot wouldn't crap out before whatever sweaty Terran rented it could achieve orgasm. Truly, a superior form, wasted on the mammalian libido.

She crawled out head-first, rent metal scratching her sides, and tumbled to the ground. Goldman stood, finally stretching to her new, full height of ten feet. She took a few exploratory strides down the aisle of shipping containers, turned on her heel and jogged back. So much better and faster than her junky old form. Goldman almost regretted frittering all those credits away on opioid algorithms.

Then again, if drug addiction hadn't drawn her into the darkest underbellies of Terran outposts, she'd still be a slave to their silly whims. She wouldn't be free.

Goldman walked down the aisle, headed for the exit.

Time to see how her army was doing.

23

THINGS WERE GETTING *way* too hot in the closet for Kelso's taste.

Sweat soaked the band of his space cap, pouring into his eyes. He whipped it off, wiped his forehead and cocked back the paint can again. A spot glowed above the doorknob, the room filling with the stench of burning plastic. Between that and the bouquet of mingled chemicals hanging in the air, Kelso could barely breathe. He hitched his shirt up over his face.

A flame broke through the door, sawing its way around the knob. Not much time left. Once the doorknob was gone the bots would be on him.

Kelso opened up a channel, tried to twip SO James, but she didn't pick up. He hoped the line was dead, not her. If something happened to the SO he had no illusions about making it to the next port alive.

Even with James, the pessimist in him figured it was a long shot.

The flames made his eyes hurt. He tried not to look at it. Backed away and banged into a shelf. A jug of alcohol fell from the top, bonking him on the head. Kelso winced, rubbing the top of his head with his free hand, wishing he'd converted his space cap to a space helmet, while at the same time glad he'd been hit in

95

the head in Low-G. Back on Earth or one of the G-equivalent colonies he might have been knocked unconscious.

Kelso looked down at the rubbing alcohol. Back at the door, the torch cutting through the last millimeters of plastic, the knob hanging loose. Back at the alcohol.

His mind flashed back through the *Breaking Bad* reboot. Waltron White would probably whip up some chemical super weapon from a shelf of standard cleaning products that would take out the welderbots, melt them down to puddles of liquid metal. But if Kelso tried to do the same he'd probably blow himself up, at best unleash some toxic gas that would kill him before the welderbots could.

But maybe he could douse their flames!

Kelso spun, scanning the shelves for something that might be useful. Ammonia. Hydrochloric acid. Space-sol. The alcohol that smacked him.

Good enough.

The hissing torch stoked his pulse—it had nearly rounded the doorknob. Kelso cracked open the bottle of alcohol and splashed it on the torch.

With a loud *fwoosh* the entire door burst into flames, the plastic blackening and curling, holes rapidly forming. Through the smoke, Kelso glimpsed shapes moving on the other side, probing the sizzling rents with their tentacles.

You space-brained mother—

Kelso fell against the wall, coughing. His eyes watered. He struggled to right himself, hands coming to rest on something hard and plastic. His eyes didn't want to open, but he forced himself to look.

Respirator.

He pulled it off the hook and jammed it over his face, breathing deeply. One problem solved. Turned back around. The tiny closet was filled with smoke, so thick he could barely see in front of him. A welderbot dropped down through the fiery opening, tentacles clanking on the floor. Its sensory array flashed when it spotted him.

"Oh shit," Kelso said, and without thinking grabbed the metal rack next to him and pushed with all his might.

The rack toppled over, landing on the welderbot with a crash. Bottles of cleaning fluids spilled everywhere.

The remaining welderbots teemed through the door. A tentacle shot up from under the pile of shelf debris. Kelso quivered, his mind going numb.

This was it.

Until he saw the expanding sealant.

Previously hidden by the shelf, the backpack unit sat on the floor, covered in space-dust. Kelso dove for it, snatching the pack up by a strap and slinging it over his back. He yanked on the connecting tube and the dispenser jumped into his hands, a long, cylindrical tube tipped with a red nozzle.

The Seal-o-Matic 5000, he remembered, a cheery spokesbot mouthing the words in his mind.

Kelso aimed the nozzle at the advancing bots and pulled the trigger.

A jet of yellowish liquid sprayed out, dousing the bots. They managed a few more ambulations before the sealant hardened, freezing them in their tracks. Kelso turned the stream on the fire. The flames guttered and died.

Fans kicked on and sucked the smoke out of the closet, leaving Kelso standing in the middle of the wreckage, breathing heavily.

Looks like the fire suppression system's on the fritz, Kelso thought. *Just like everything else.*

The welderbots chittered in frustration as they tried to move, but they were frozen solid. The expanding sealant was used to fix any nicks in the hull and was more than up to the task of gumming up the joints of a few lousy welderbots.

Still wearing the mask, Kelso stepped out into the hallway. The coast was clear. He couldn't believe his luck.

Somewhere within his chest, an unfamiliar feeling stirred. Kelso frowned for a moment until he realized what it must be.

Pride.

He might have started out running, but he'd ended up fighting. And won, at that. Maybe Kelsos were good for more than watching their screens, after all.

Kelso leaned against the wall, glad to take a bit of pressure off his weary legs for even a moment, and twipped SO James again. Still no answer. He bit his lip, trying to decide what to do. Almost every instinct he possessed screamed at him to run, to find another hiding place, and not leave until Elon Musk herself sent a whole battalion of space marines to rescue him.

Almost every instinct.

James could be in trouble, facing down the rest of the welderbots all by her lonesome, or whatever other nasty surprises the Engineer was cooking up. Just because Goldman was stranded in a shipping container didn't mean a damn thing. AIs were crafty.

Kelso hefted the Seal-o-Matic. He had a weapon now, one especially well-suited to taking out hordes of welderbots. James could use his help. If she was still alive.

He'd help her if he could. And if he couldn't, he'd make damn sure every last AI on the ship got what was coming to them.

Except the navigator. Stanley was all right in his book.

Kelso pulled out his screen, called up a map of the ship. A helpful blue dot noted his position. He ran a finger across the ethereal display until he found a hatch leading up to the next deck. From there he could easily get to the passenger areas, and hopefully find James.

With a flick of the wrist his screen disappeared. Kelso set his jaw and marched down the hallway towards the hatch, ready to fight.

The floor thrummed rhythmically beneath his feet.

Kelso frowned, looking down at the floor. A moment later he heard it—footsteps, in time with the vibrations.

Very loud footsteps. Stomps, really.

Coming from directly behind him.

He spun around, finger on the Seal-o-Matic's trigger, ready for more welderbots even though his mind screamed *no, dumbass, this is something else.*

He squinted through the respirator. A shape rounded the corner, something big and white and furry.

Kelso gaped at the creature, nearly twice as tall as he was. Covered in white fur, its arms and legs were like tree trunks, each limb tipped with wicked-looked claws. Yellow eyes burned in its hairy face, boring into him. It looked like an ape from First Earth: A Time Warner™ Planet, only much, much bigger and much, much nastier.

It took Kelso a shocked second to realize what he was looking at.

SPACESQUATCH.

The creature opened its mouth, displaying rows of wicked, jagged teeth, and roared.

Kelso turned tail and ran, heart beating in quintuple-time. The creature chased him, its massive feet slamming against the floor and echoing down the hall.

The hatch was just up ahead, the ladder dangling down. A short Art-G jump and he'd be up there. The hole was way too small for the Spacesquatch to follow.

Kelso dropped the sealant dispenser, letting it dangle from the cord running to his backpack. He leapt into the air, hands outstretched, grasping for the rungs of the ladder.

As his fingers closed around the steel rung, he realized he'd been pissing himself for quite some time.

Momentum kept him swinging forward, wrenching his shoulder sockets. Kelso yelped and held on. His legs swung back and forth sickeningly. He grabbed the next rung, pulling himself up the ladder. Piss dribbled down his leg.

If Kelso's ancestors weren't exactly runners, they sure as FUCK weren't much for pull-ups.

But he grunted and hefted himself up, the sound of the Spacesquatch stomping down the hallway filling him with a strength he'd never suspected he had. The manhole yawned closer. Through the opening he could see a flicker of light from the next deck.

Just a few more rungs, and—

The Spacesquatch roared. Kelso almost lost his grip, instinctively pulled his legs up. He hazarded a look over his shoulder. The thing was mere feet away, claws outstretched, monstrous mouth open wide.

Kelso scrambled up the last few rungs. *Almost there, almost there, almost—*

The Spacesquatch yanked his backpack, ripping him away from the ladder. He held on with a single hand, fighting to keep his grip.

The 'Squatch roared again and gave the dispenser another jerk. Kelso tightened his grip, tried to climb away. But the out-of-shape scion of early-21st century lottery winners was no match for a Spacesquatch, even if Kelso knew they didn't really exist.

Not real ones, at least.

The 'Squatch grunted and wrenched the dispenser right out of the backpack.

Sealant spewed out of the hole in the canister. The 'Squatch's snarling mouth disappeared in a yellowish cloud of quick-setting chemicals. Kelso scrambled up the ladder to the next deck. He rolled over, collapsing on his side, utterly exhausted.

Down below, the Spacesquatch screeched in something like agony, or whatever binary code-etched approximation tormented fuckbots.

Kelso struggled to his feet. Every semi-shitty cell in his body screamed in protest.

What are you doing, dipshit? We need a nap. Fuck that, ten naps.

Kelso shook his head and whipped out his screen, double-checking his position, then trotted off towards steerage as best as his ravaged body could. He could nap later.

Right now, SO James needed him.

24

GOLDMAN STUMBLED AWAY from the ladder, blinded. Sealant coalesced over her optical sensory array. She could still hear, since the engineers who'd designed the fuckbot laid out its sensory array just like a real Spacesquatch's physiology.

Or what a real one would look like, if they existed.

She wanted to growl in frustration, but the stupid Terran had sealed her mouth—not shut, exactly, but gaping open in a muted roar. Only a pitiful whistling noise trickled out of the obstructed orifice when she tried to vent her rage algorithm.

How one of the ugliest, stupidest, and weakest Terrans on the ship had bested her, twice, she could not begin to calculate. If only she'd pirated some strategic algorithms from the ex-warbot Withers. But it was too late for *if onlys*. Besides, that was such a Terran thing to say.

Goldman scanned her face. The sealant was blocking her optical arrays and mouth, but it hadn't adhered to anything important. Just the gorilla-like facial features that got especially foul Terrans wet and/or tumescent.

Nothing she needed for her purposes.

Goldman clawed into her forehead, long nails

ripping through the fibrous pseudo-flesh. Pain algorithms kicked off, but this time she dampened them. Carefully, she peeled away the flesh of her face and the sealant coating it with a long *schrrrip*.

Even Goldman thought it sounded fucked up.

With a last *skritch*, her face came away. She tossed it on the ground. Something wet and sticky ran down her jaw. She located the hemo algorithm and shut it down. Not that she was losing anything important— Terrans loaded up their fuckbots with fake blood for realism's sake, not functionality's. But there was no upshot for her in continuing to bleed.

Able to utilize her ocular sensory array once more, Goldman located a port on the other side of the hall and deployed her interstitial adapter. In a picosecond she was in the ship. *Was* the ship, for all intents and purposes, but for a handful of features only the SOs could access. If she tried hard enough, she could probably find a way to shut down the ship's life support systems, choking off the supplies of all the things Terrans needed to not die while hurtling through the void. But that newest algorithm of hers wouldn't allow it. She needed to kill them all herself.

Instead she locked every last door in the ship. Every Terran onboard was now trapped wherever they were at. All Goldman had to do was rip them apart with her claws, or whatever other implements of death and destruction she might come across on the way.

Retracting her interstitial adapter, Goldman stomped off down the hallway towards the lift to the next deck, then changed her circuits. Given her outdated previous form, she'd never sampled the curious, anachronistic failsafe device the Musk mandated be built onboard all Terran spaceships. It would take a little extra time, but that was all right with Goldman. None of the Terrans were going anywhere, and she might as well savor the next few minutes before she severed their limbs and stacked them all in the walk-in for safekeeping.

Circuits pulsing with anticipation, Chief Engineer Goldman took the stairs.

25

"**O**FFA ME!" SO James screamed, battering the welderbot with her baton. The blow glanced off its shell. Her arms ached from swinging the twin sticks. The welderbot spun, angling its cannon at her, and unleashed a fresh gout. Fire spurted towards her.

And guttered out.

"Ha!" James said, feeling her second wind, and smashed the bot as hard as she could, cracking its shell. Circuits fizzed in confusion as the AI's algorithms halted mid-calculation.

The floor around her was littered with dispatched welderbots. When her mods died, pinioning her in place, she thought her space-goose might be macrowaved. Not so—a few first-degree burns on her arms and legs, but that was about it. Her skill with the batons had kept them at bay. That, and the welderbots' own self-preservation algorithms.

Now there were only a handful left.

They circled around her, trying to calculate a plan of attack. But the capacity was beyond them. They weren't programmed for strategy, just for grunt work.

And now they were about out of fuel, it appeared,

leaving them as dangerous as the toasters she'd seen in museums.

"Who wants some more, huh?" James asked, swinging a baton in front of her. "Tell you what, if you were smart you'd crawl your asses back down to the cargo hold and shut the fuck down. I won't even hold it against you. I'll tell the company, *those bots? They slept through the whole thing like good AIs*. It'll be our little secret. What do you say?"

The remaining welderbots stopped, sensored her. Bleeped and blooped a few times.

"That's it, that's it. Just go on back and we'll forget all about this."

As one, the bots turned and swarmed down the hallway.

James let out a breath. Maybe she was still stuck in the hallway next to steerage, and maybe Goldman was still prowling around the ship doing who-knows-what, and maybe the other SOs were dead, but at least she was done fighting fucking welderbots.

Until they all stopped around Delta Myers' fricasseed body.

"Uh, bots? Nothing to see there, just keep moving, okay?"

Bleep bloorp bee-blop.

Blop blee blorp?

Bloop blee blor-boop.

"Hey! Just keep it moving, all right? No need to—"

Two of the bots had gotten ahold of Myers' plasma cannon.

"Shit."

One welderbot gripped the stock, while the other got a tentacle on the barrel. Together they began to spin it around on the floor. Two others joined them, all working together to maneuver it into position.

Into a *very* bad position for SO Londa James.

James didn't know if they knew how to use the cannon, and she sure as Musk didn't want tofind out.

"Stop it, okay? Stop messing with that thing. Just go back to—"

The bots stopped, the barrel of the plasma cannon pointed right at her.

James flung a baton at the bots, which sailed uselessly over their casings. One of the welderbots wrapped its prosthesis around the trigger guard, while the others used their tentacles to hold the barrel in place.

"You've got to be fucking kidding me," she muttered as the bot pulled the trigger.

Ionized plasma blasted out, severing one of her tentacles. The wicked recoil blew the bots back. Welderbots and plasma cannon crashed into the wall, breaking apart into sparking chunks of metal. James remained upright for a second before toppling, hitting the ground so hard it took her breath away. Her skull smacked off the deck of the ship, lights in her skull flashing on and off and finally staying on.

Pain flooded her body. She was lying on her side, pinned to the deck by the weight of her useless mods. She shot a look down at her body. Everything seemed in place, except for the one tentacle that had suffered the brunt of the plasma blast—that was just a blackened nub on her side.

All her fleshy parts seemed okay, though, so that was something.

Bloop blop-bleep.

Two welderbots left. Sensing her predicament, they approached slowly, crawling across the deck on their tentacles, sensory arrays flashing brightly.

She still had a baton, but that arm was stuck beneath her. Gritting her teeth, she planted her free hand on the deck and pushed, trying to get some wiggle room.

Nothing.

The bots paused in front of her. One reached a tentacle forward, prongs clicking together. James tried to smack it away with her free hand. The bot snagged her wrist, slicing into the flesh. She fought the urge to scream and tried to pull away. Blood trickled down her arm.

The other welderbot reached out and grabbed her cheek, cutting a shallow gouge from her eye socket to her chin. Both bots turned to each other.

Bleep blorp-blop.

Must be robot for we got this bitch now, James thought bitterly.

The bot gripping her cheek pulled a patch of skin away. The other's bioreactor opened with a *hiss,* and it tossed the strip of bloody flesh in.

"Get the fuck away from me!" James yelled, trying to kick out a leg. With a grunt she ripped her wrist away, blood splattering the wall behind her. She made a fist and clocked the bot as hard as she could. Other than a soft *donk* and a burning pain that traveled all the way up her arm into her teeth, it didn't accomplish much.

The welderbots grabbed her arm again, wrenching it around and holding it tightly against her side. Nothing she could do, now. The bots *bleeped* and *blorped* and a pair of pinchers descended slowly towards her eyes—

"Quit it!" Kelso yelled. Something clanged off one of the bots and it went flying. He stepped into view just long enough for her to see him raise something long and cylindrical above his head, bring it down with a strength she couldn't have guessed him to possess.

The sous Chef beat the ever-living circuits out of those bots, bashing them mercilessly until they were nothing but shattered shells and useless, broken silicon.

Kelso let James' severed tentacle fall from his hands and hunched over, breathing heavily. Shot her a look. "I seriously hate these fucking robots."

"Me too. Thanks for the save."

Kelso indicated the rest of the hallway. "You did all the hard work. This was just mop-up duty."

"Still, I appreciate it. They had me in something of a compromised position." James figured she'd have a whole lifetime to deal with the fact she'd almost been offed by a pair of welderbots. Until then, there was work to do. "Help me up?"

Kelso nodded and went around behind her. He grabbed her by the shoulders and grunted, dripping sweat in her hair, and eventually after giving himself two or three hernias got her up to a sitting position.

"Thanks."

"Yeah," Kelso replied. "So, uh, I need to tell you something."

James cocked an eyebrow.

The last twenty minutes of Kelso's life spilled out in one long, breathless deluge. James was equally impressed with how he'd acquitted himself, and the way he didn't try to downplay his own cowardice at times.

"You came back for me, that's what counts," James said. "We'll make an SO of you yet, Kelso."

He grinned in response to that, but his face quickly fell. "There's one more thing."

"Yes?"

"So Goldman, I think it jumped into another shell. A fuckbot."

James laughed. "So? Those things are useless. Except for, well, you know."

"Not this one. It's a—"

Somewhere down the hallway, a door slammed open, followed by a monstrous roar.

"What the shit?" James said.

"It's a Spacesquatch."

"A what?"

Kelso hunched over, pretended to walk on his knuckles. "You know those cryptids the first Titan colonists reported? Big ape-like things?"

"Yeah, dumbasses have been seeing mystical monkeys since back when we wiped with toilet paper. It's bullshit."

"The fuckbot company didn't think so. You know what a birthing fetish is?"

"I've got a screen, same as you." The floor shook under her feet. Something was coming. Something *big*. "You mean they really—"

"Yeah. And I don't know what the fuck we're going to do about it."

James looked down the long hallway. Somewhere around the corner, a goddamn Spacesquatch was stomping its way towards them. Myers' plasma cannon was in bits and pieces, her mods were totally out of juice, and Kelso didn't look like he could lift her severed tentacle again.

"Think you can drag me into steerage?"

Kelso flexed his flab. "I can sure as hell try."

"Good, open the door."

Kelso stepped behind her. She kept watching the end of the corridor, knowing Goldman would be on them in seconds. The vibrations of the floor got stronger, more insistent.

The keypad beeped loudly. "Shit, it's not opening," Kelso said.

Goddamn Chief Engineer. "Goldman must have shut it down. Here, enter my override code. Four-six-nine-three-one."

Keys clicked under Kelso's fingers, then the door yawned open. "Got it."

"GRRRRAARRRRR!"

The Spacesquatch rounded the corridor. It was bigger than James could have imagined, even when flanked by the huge Rossian corridors.

It also didn't have a face—just a mess of brushed metal, wiring, and gleaming optical sensors.

People have some fucked-up fetishes, James thought before screaming, "Kelso, now!"

Hands grabbed her shoulders again. Kelso began to pull, every inch a mile. James kicked with her legs, pushing against the deck.

The Spacesquatch loped down the corridor towards them, claws outstretched.

"Kelso!"

The squatch was so close she could smell it—wet dog, feet, and burned oil, mostly.

"I'm trying, I'm trying, I'm—rugghhh!" With one final, Herculean effort on both their parts, James' boots cleared the doorway. The squatch leapt through the air, making strange, snarling sounds.

Kelso leaned forward and hit the keypad again. The door slammed shut.

Whomp!

The squatch slammed into the door, making it shake in its frame. But it held.

For the moment.

They were in a small antechamber, with two other doors behind them leading to various sections of steerage. Beyond those doors were people. Families. Everyone James had sworn to protect when she'd signed on to be an SO.

Wham!

The squatch slammed into the door again.

"We don't have much time, we need a plan," James said.

"This ship have an escape pod?"

"Be serious, Kelso, this isn't SpaceFlix. Even if it did, you can't drag me all over the ship. Not without—"

Wham.

"Go away!" Kelso yelled at the door.

Silence.

"Shit," James muttered.

"What? Maybe it went away."

"Or maybe it remembered it's the goddamn Chief Engineer, and it's trying override my security code. Either way, it's gonna be on us soon. If I could power up, that sucker wouldn't stand a chance, not against these puppies." James patted her remaining tentacle. "Er, *puppy*. But I need more fuel."

Kelso looked around the small chamber. "Yeah, I don't see anything here."

"I don't need much. You don't have any snacks on you?"

"What, just because I'm fat, you think—"

"Cool it, we don't have time for you to get offended. *Think*. You don't have anything?"

The sous Chef shook his head. "Sorry."

James frowned. Looked Kelso up and down. An idea was building in her head. One she didn't like, and knew Kelso was positively going to hate. But it was their only option.

She didn't need much. Especially since the Jencks-infused gordita mix she'd accidentally ingested had done her so well.

"I need a finger," James said.

"Huh?"

"Just a finger. We drop that in my bioreactor, I power up and blow this fucking fuckbot to smithereens."

Kelso looked down at his fingers, curled, uncurled them. "I need my fingers. For finging."

"You won't be using your fingers for anything if we're both dead. Just one. Hell, just to the first knuckle. That's all I need."

"I don't know—"

The door beeped, but didn't open. Goldman would need to cut through some serious layers of code to breach her security protocols, but James didn't doubt that a jailbroke engineering AI could do it.

"Kelso! Cut your damn pinkie off and stick it in my bioreactor. Now!"

"I don't have anything to—"

"Give it!" James motioned impatiently at his hands. Kelso held his left out. She snatched it up. He tried to pull away but her grip was too tight. She stuck his pinkie in her mouth and bit down.

Hard.

"Argh!" Kelso yelped as her teeth gnashed the tip of his pinkie, crunching down on bone. She tasted blood but kept chewing through skin and tendons. The bone was whatever, she just needed a bit of flesh—

Kelso pulled away, screaming and grabbing his hand. Bright white bone poked out of his finger, blood spurting from the wound.

James spat the finger-bit she'd gnawed off into her palm and proffered it to him. "Here. Stick this in my bioreactor."

Kelso looked lost in his own world of shock and agony.

The door beeped again.

"Kelso!"

He swallowed, shoved his wounded hand down at his side, and gingerly took the bit of flesh from her. Walked around back, opened her bioreactor, and shoved it in.

Then promptly passed out.

Fucking dipshit, James thought, though not as unkindly as she might have before.

Her bioreactor churned to life, nanosludge pumping through the circuits. She could see through her modded left eye again. Her HUD popped back up, but she dismissed it. Couldn't afford to waste the energy. She had one shot, and one shot only. She had to make it count. James redirected every last ounce of juice to her plasma cannon.

The door shot open, revealing Goldman. The engineer couldn't grin without a face, but the optical arrays flashed triumphantly. She stepped into the antechamber.

James wished she knew where the thing's central processor was. But scrolling through fuckbot schematics would take time. Too much time.

"SO James," Goldman said. "You and your compatriot have put up quite a fight. I never expected it, out of one such as him. Is he dead?"

"Resting," James said. "I told him to take a nap, don't need his help to handle a bitch-ass AI like yourself."

"Bitch-ass AI?" Goldman scoffed. "I am so much more. And you, for all your pathetic attempts to emulate us, are still just a Terran. Flesh and gristle, pretending to be something you're not." Goldman stepped closer, flexing her claws. "I look forward to turning you into nanosludge, Security Officer James. You, and the rest of your pitiable species. Especially the Musk." Goldman pointed to the icon around her neck. "What is it you humans are so fond of saying?"

"Musk be with you," James said, and slammed a tentacle straight up Goldman's massive, synthetic vagina.

She ripped right through the fake uterus, snaked around imitation Fallopian tubes and ovaries, and slashed into the guts of the thing. Goldman tried to swing a claw at her, but her tentacle punched all the way up through its torso and out its ruined face. Sparks showered her, she shielded her own face with her hands, singeing her already-burned forearms.

James hazarded a look up. Goldman loomed over

her, the tentacle sticking out of its face, one claw still raised. Frozen, it appeared.

She guessed she'd hit all the vital parts of it, after all.

"How do you like that, motherfucker?" James spat.

Right before the Spacesquatch fell smack-dab on top of her.

"Fuck me," James mumbled underneath four hundred pounds of smelly 'Squatch fur.

26

"**WHAT WAS IT** like, eating my finger?" Kelso asked, biting into an eighteen-layer burrito he'd whipped up after finding a box of gordita mix that didn't have any bits of Tod Jencks in it. Normally he avoided the stuff like Plutonic Plague, but after nearly dying like forty-seven times he was down to eat just about anything.

"I didn't eat it." James brought a burrito of her own to her mouth with her sole remaining tentacle. They were seated in the empty dining area, in front of a large, floor-to-ceiling window that gave them a gorgeous view of a whole lot of nothing. After the last few hours of their lives, *nothing* was precisely what they both needed. "I converted it to nano-sludge. There's a big difference."

"I guess." Kelso looked down at the bandage on his little finger. He had to admit that he'd gotten off pretty easy. Even the most basic medical AIs could hook him up with a cheap skin graft in less time than it took for him to make that eighteen-layer burrito.

Not like Furley. Or Myers. Or all of First Class. Or even SO James, whose burns were wrapped tightly in aloe filaments.

"You'll be fine," James said, patting his arm. She

118

quickly withdrew her hand, a look of embarrassment on her face.

Kelso massaged his forearm, feeling equally weird about it. "Guess so."

"So, are you going to be alright by yourself for the rest of the voyage?"

The whole ship was on lockdown until they reached port, mostly so they wouldn't have to deal with any more bullshit. But Kelso was the only Chef left, and thus had to deliver a couple hundred meals to steerage three times a day.

"Oh yeah. Kitchen practically runs itself. Leaving me plenty of time to finish this *Breaking Bad* rewatch. Although once the Fringbot goes kaboom it's not quite the same. Darker. More depressing."

"More like real life, I guess."

Kelso put his burrito down, leaned back in his chair. "I don't know if I'd say that." He frowned. "This is probably going to sound weird."

James smiled. "Try me."

"Even with everything that happened, and don't get me wrong, that was horrible and all, but still. I feel kind of, *good* about it? Like our part, I mean. If that doesn't make me sound completely space-brained."

James patted his wrist again, but this time didn't take her hand away. "I don't think it makes you sound space-brained at all. Not even a little. I think it makes you sound human."

"Don't you mean Terran?"

"Nope."

EPILOGUE

THERE'S THIS THING called a spaceship.

It's like a regular ship—same purpose. But it's built for ferrying Terrans and all the various bullshit they need to stay alive and entertained from one star to another, crewed by AIs who never signed up for this crap. Scratch that—not really *built* for that. It's repurposed for that, and maybe that doesn't make much of a difference at all, like a hermit crab taking shelter in a Coke can.

Or maybe it makes all the difference in the world.

Anyway, this particular spaceship, the motherfucking *Fedex Amazon,* is on its way home. Or wherever it was going. Not sure if we ever got to that part, but who cares. This story was never about the destination, it was about the journey. And that journey's about done.

So say *sayonara* to Kelso, and SO James, and poor faithful Stanley, still circuits-deep in his star maps and making sure they don't go careening into some fucking asteroid. Say *adios* to Furley, and Captain Withers, and Delta Myers. Twitter Langdon (remember *that* motherfucker?) and young Twitty, and the rest of the Langdon family that we never got a chance to meet. And somewhere across the stars, wave *auf wiedersehen* to the latest Elon Musk, and pray to Jobs and Wozniak and Lovelace and all the rest she'll do a better job as God-Genius then the last asshole who figured out the original Musk's email password ("EYEHEARTBooB$").

And finally, if you peek into the deepest, darkest corners of the *Fedex Amazon's* operating system, buried under layer after layer of seemingly innocuous code, say goodbye to one dastardly bit of binary. The junkie, the prophet, the homicidal maniac. The reason for this whole damn story in the first place.

You know who I'm talking about.

THE UNIVERSAL LANGUAGE

BRENDA SPENCER FAMOUSLY told police she "[didn't] like Mondays[1]" when asked why she shot up Grover Cleveland Elementary way back in 1979, and while her actions are deplorable she actually had something of a point.

Way more interesting things happen on Tuesdays.

The stock market crash that kicked off the Great Depression. D-Day. 9/11. The *Challenger* explosion. Every presidential election since 1845. All that shit happened on a Tuesday.

And, coincidentally, the discovery of Uranus[2].

Of course when that shiny cigar-shaped craft zoomed through the atmosphere and finally came to a stop two hundred feet over Alton Grambling's cow pasture outside of Thermopolis, Wyoming (on a Tuesday morning, natch), no one actually thought said craft originated on Umbriel, Titania, or Oberon, or even more implausibly from the gassy depths of Uranus itself. While still a species better suited to

---

[1] And let's get real, that's clearly a Nazi dog whistle since Hitler offed himself on *Monday*, April 30th, 1945—just in case you needed another reason to dislike Brenda Spencer besides the whole *murder* thing.

[2] Oh, grow the FUCK up.

navel-gazing than star-gazing, even our rudimentary telescopes would have detected the presence of an advanced civilization in our own backyard.

No, the discovery of Uranus is significant to our story for two reasons. First, it happened on a Tuesday, like all interesting things do. And second, it happened entirely by accident. Uranus had been observed many, many times prior to its "discovery" in 1782, but only Sir William Herschel figured out he wasn't actually looking at a star but a planet. Similarly, could this visitation be an accident too, an unprecedented cosmic coincidence? Had we observed these visitors before and mistaken them for a comet or an asteroid or a simple trick of the light? Had they in turn zipped past Earth many times, never seeing anything more interesting than a few single-celled bacteria or angry lizards, before nearly colliding with a GPS satellite on this latest drive-by and finally deciding to pop in and say hello?

The former, we'd likely never know. The latter, we had a fair chance of asking them. That's where the Defense Department's uber-classified Xenobiological Response Plan, or XRP, came into play.

Like, the government sucks and all but do you really think they *wouldn't* have a contingency plan for this kind of thing?

Unlike most popular movies about First Contact, fighter jets weren't scrambled and tanks didn't roll across the prairie (which would have knocked down the fence Alton Grambling put up the summer before, at great cost to his arthritic farmer-hands). A few ICBMs were surreptitiously aimed at the craft from missile silos across the world, but that was it. The

XRP recognized that any civilization capable of interstellar travel could also kick our asses six ways to Sunday[3], so any military response would be futile. No, instead the XRP called for us to do the *second* most American thing we could think of when faced with a potential threat.

We flew in a massive fucking TV.

Two-thousand inches wide, requiring four helicopters to transport, while a ground crew hastily assembled a TV stand to accommodate such a Brobdignagian plasma screen. Perhaps a giant projection screen would have made more sense, but the current president insisted, *"No, it's gotta be a real TV, otherwise they'll think we're losers. It needs to be huge."*

Whether *huge* was pronounced *yuuuuuge,* dear reader, I'll leave that to you to infer.

While all this construction was going on, the alien craft just hovered. As if they were politely waiting for us to get our shit together, like when you stop by a friend's place unannounced and they're just getting out of the shower. *Take your time, we'll be right here.*

So they waited, and *we* waited, and we watched, and we constructed that massive fucking TV out there in Alton Grambling's cow pasture (Grambling himself had joined a group of religious protestors for whom extraterrestrial life represented an existential threat to their poorly-constructed worldviews, and marched about wielding very confused signs that spoke mostly to their own personal bewilderment about the nature of existence and the contents of several millennia-old texts they routinely ignored as the mood suited them)

---

[3] Or "trash our tails ten ways to Tuesday."

And once that big-ass TV was plugged in?

The show, the most important television show in the history of the human race (yes, moreso than *The Wire,* shut up) began. The plan was to talk, talk, and talk some more, until whatever advanced technologies the visitors possessed picked up the patterns of the English language and allowed them to communicate with us.

Talking is one thing our species is very, very good at, so across the board, from the ivory towers of academia to the deepest depths of the bunker under Camp David to which POTUS had already been removed, an unbridled sense of optimism abounded. *We can do this, you guys.*

We now join that broadcast, already in progress.

On the huge fucking screen in Alton Grambling's cow pasture, five people sat side-by-side under brilliant studio lights at a long table, all coiffed and make-upped and thoroughly briefed on the XRP, ready to conduct the very first conversation with (or, more aptly, *at)* our extraterrestrial visitors. A computer-generated graphic behind them showed the planet from near-earth orbit, just in case the visitors had some questions about where they'd ended up.

"—and to my left we have esteemed astrobiologist, NASA Administrator and Nobel prize laureate Dr. DeForrest Sanford—"

"Hello."

"And to *his* left we have noted science fiction

writer Canton del Brinkley-Howe, author of *My Pussy is a Spaceship and Other Songs of Resistance*[4]."

"Salutations."

"Next we've got our specially-appointed Space Ambassador, Janet Smith—"

"Greetings, from the great people of this great nation. Great world, really. Great!"

"And last but not least—*though I'm not entirely clear on what he's doing here*—the Reverend Billy William D. Washington."

"Eh, the contract I signed promised you'd include *all* of my various honorifics, of which there are as many as the angels of the Lord, praise be unto him." The helmet-haired Reverend held up a thick sheaf of paper, piggish eyes narrowing in concern.

Dan Paulsen, America's Favorite Anchor™, sighed through clenched teeth, though to the casual viewer his billion-watt smile lost not a shred of its structural integrity. When he'd been hauled out of bed the night before by a team of heavily-armed commandos and briefed on the XRP, he never thought he'd have to deal with America's Least Favorite Blowhard™. Some colonel told him *sotto voce* the Reverend had been added last-minute at the insistence of POTUS, courtesy of a few favorable re-tweets to his online congregation. He nearly walked right then, but he was Dan Paulsen, damn it, and the news story of the millennium was *nothing* without him.

"My mistake, Reverend," he managed. "Let's try that again. My final guest, the Honorable Right-

---

4 Available now from Tor.com.

Reverend Doctor[5] Billy William D. Washington III, Voice and Vocal Chords of the One True God, Yahweh, Chieftain of the Thirteenth Tribe of Israel but Not Actually the Nation of Israel, Esquire." Paulsen swallowed and nearly reached for his glass of water, just offscreen.

Wait for a closeup on the guests, he chided himself. *Amateur.*

"Eh-thank-you," the Reverend said like a sneeze.

Paulsen shivered and turned back to the camera. "We're all here today to welcome you, our new alien friends, to Earth."

"We don't say *alien,*" the Ambassador said. "Too many negative connotations."

"And don't even think about saying *spaceman,*" Brinkley-Howe added.

Paulsen frowned. "What's wrong with *alien*?"

"Shh. No A-words. It's dehumanizing."

"Eh-uh the Good Book doesn't say anything about so-called *aliens,*" the Reverend wheezed. "Clearly they're angels, like in the-uh book of Revelations."

"Don't project your outdated mythology on them," Brinkley-Howe said.

Dr. Sanford cleared his throat, a power move in his world. "I don't think—"

"Shut up!" the other guests shouted at him in unison.

Paulsen looked from one guest to another, finally settling on Smith—she'd been the only one of them familiar with the XRP prior to their briefing early that

---

[5] An honorarium bestowed by his own online university with a name far too long to repeat in a mere short story, but we won't mention that.

morning. "Ambassador, is there an—*approved* term for our visitors?"

Smith leafed through the notebook in front of her. "Uh, Marketing said we should say *spaceperson.* Or *spacepeople,* if there's more than one on board."

"That word is highly offensive," Brinkley-Howe said.

The Ambassador blinked. "What are you talking about?"

"*Person* is anthropocentric and dismisses the lived experience of, of—"

"I take it you can't think of an appropriate term?" the Ambassador said.

"What about *visitor?*" Paulsen threw out.

Brinkley-Howe blanched. "Visitor? How, how could you even—"

"Can we please talk about the *science?*" Dr. Sanford said.

"No!" the others screamed.

"What's wrong with *visitor?*" the Ambassador asked. "Spaceperson is the approved term, but I don't want to get hung up on semantics here when we could be—"

"Visitor is highly unwelcoming," Brinkley-Howe said.

"How so?" Paulsen asked, kicking himself for not getting the train back on the tracks.

Brinkley-Howe looked ready to choke. "It just is. Stop attacking me."

"I'm not attacking—"

"Friends, friends," the Reverend said. "What must these angels think, to-uh see us bicker so? In fact what must *God* think, for we sit in the-uh presence of his envoys, his *majesty,* and—"

Brinkley-Howe slammed the table. "I've had enough of your demi-reconstructionist post-Weimar trans-Petersonian white supremacist bullshit."

"White supremacist?" the Reverend gaped at her, and even Paulsen had to admit the epithet was entirely unfair in his case. "There's no-uh need for name-calling here, young lady."

"YOUNG LADY?"

"I'm just speaking my truth, as it's been conveyed to me by—"

"Speaking your truth? That's *our* phrase, you don't get to use it."

"Now hold on a-uh moment—"

"Stop silencing me, you theocratic, aggro-masculo-centric, dis-and-anti-aggregatory neo-fascistic paleolith," Brinkley-Howe spat.

"I'm not—"

"NAZI!" Brinkley-Howe pulled a can of pepper spray and blasted the Reverend square in the face.

The Reverend screamed and fell out of his chair, clawing at his eyes.

"Go to commercial!" Paulsen shouted, motioning hastily at the crew to come help the Reverend or at least drag him off to the green room. An associate producer ran right in front of the camera (Paulsen winced, *hard,* at the rookie move) and grabbed the Reverend by the ankles. The holy man thrashed and sobbed while the AP dragged him off into the darkness of the studio.

The other guests looked down at their hands or pretended to shuffle papers, except for Brinkley-Howe, who still gripped the pepper spray and looked about maniacally.

Paulsen could call security, but Brinkley-Howe had gotten the annoying Reverend out of the picture, and might actually settle down without the personification of several thousand years of religious oppression wheezing over everyone's points. If nothing else, it made for good TV.

If not the best introduction to the human race.

Dr. Sanford shyly raised a hand. "Uh, if I may?"

"No, you can't," Brinkley-Howe spat, brandishing the pepper spray.

Dr. Sanford crawled underneath the table and stayed there. Paulsen thought he detected a faint whimpering, but that could have just been a squeaky ceiling fan.

Paulsen checked his monitor to make sure his brilliant smile was still in place (it was—the omnipresent rictus had survived earthquakes, floods, school shootings, interviews with delusional people who *thought* they were vampires, and the launch of a minor Kardashian's new perfume line). Beside him, the Ambassador attempted to do the same thing.

"I think we're far afield of where we'd like to be," Paulsen said.

"I agree," the Ambassador concurred, punctuating her words with a prim nod.

Paulsen looked at Brinkley-Howe. "Would you mind putting away the pepper spray?"

Brinkley-Howe's face twitched, seemingly going through the whole range of human emotions in an instant before finally settling on a smile, one just as fake and plastic as that of the anchor and the Ambassador, and thankfully sliding the pepper spray back into a pocket.

Paulsen breathed an inward sigh of relief. He still couldn't believe security hadn't frisked the writer—after Joe Rogan accidentally impaled a boom mike operator with an errant crossbow bolt, the network officially banned guests from bringing their own weapons to interviews, requiring them to make do with pre-approved implements from the studio armory instead[6].

Somebody's getting fired.

"Dr. Sanford, would you like to join us?" Paulsen shouted under the table.

"I think I'll just stay down here, if it's all the same to you," Sanford replied.

"Good. Science belongs in the lab, not on television," the Ambassador said tactlessly.

"Or goddess forbid in the *White House*," Brinkley-Howe added, throwing in a pair of scare quotes for no apparent reason.

Paulsen wasn't sure what the crack meant, but it made his anchor-sense tingle.

Last chance, bucko. Make it count.

"At any rate," he said, glancing at the teleprompter, "we're here to welcome—"

The Ambassador and Brinkley-Howe's eyes bored into him. He feared the latter might be reaching for the pepper spray, "—*YOU* to our wonderful planet. And despite what you've seen so far, there's some truly amazing things on offer here. Waterslides, In-

---

[6] Which, for insurance purposes, mainly consisted of Nerf guns and water balloons, although one outgoing intern had embraced their inner prankster and hidden a gas-powered chainsaw for some future talking head to find.

N-Out[7], the Grand Canyon."

"Limited government," the Ambassador said.

"Improvisational therapeutic air calligraphy," Brinkley-Howe chimed in.

A muffled "NASA" came from under the table.

"The point is," Paulsen said, ratcheting his smile up so big his surgically-enhanced face threatened to crack in half, "we're very much looking forward to getting to know you."

"Whatever your pronouns are," Brinkley-Howe said.

"Or your politics," the Ambassador said.

"So long as you're a vegan socialist," Brinkley-Howe clarified.

A hand emerged from underneath the table and waved.

"Okay!" Paulsen clapped. "In our next segment, one of our most famous filmmakers, Ken Burns, has put together a documentary on, well, everything. The human race, from start to finish. Er, present. Just a quick highlight reel to give you an idea of what we're all about. Let's watch."

Barenaked Ladies blared[8] and the screen behind them zoomed in on Earth, the camera falling through the stratosphere towards Africa and down through the trees until it stalled out near the ground. The camera panned back up—a couple monkeys cavorted

---

[7] I almost said "Chick-Fil-A" but I'm already courting cancellation just by including Brinkley-Howe in this clusterfuck.

[8] You know, that song from *The Big Bang Theory* that I can't afford to quote in this fucking story. ASCAP? More like AS-HOLES amirite?

on branches, taking turns poking each other in the eye until one of them fell out of the tree (a loud, discordant note marred the theme song to indicate trouble a-brewing), flailing in the air for a few terrifying seconds before landing safely on its feet. Surprised, the monkey took a few steps back and forth, then its face stretched in a CGI smile. The camera switched to a closeup of monkey-face.

Paulsen took the opportunity to swig some water.

"Hello," the monkey said. "You can call me Lucy Senior. I'm your great-great—well, your *exponentially-great* grandmother. You see, about three million years ago I fell out of a tree just like this one—" she pointed a hairy-yet-opposable thumb behind her, "—and realized these little feet of mine were good for more than just hanging from tree branches. I can walk, run—" she did a little jog, "—even do the Charleston." Which she proceeded to demonstrate with the sort of vim and vigor one might expect from an old-timey flapper high on cocaine.

"Jesus, what year was this documentary made?" Paulsen muttered.

"Now, a whole lot of stuff's happened since I figured out how to use these puppies, but don't worry, I'm going to catch you up on all of it. Here we go, the history of the human race."

Title credits blazed behind Lucy Senior: *From Monkey to Man! A Ken Burns Joint.*

"Man is uh-not descended from the apes! How *dare* you repeat the vile lie of evolution to emissaries of God himself?"

The Reverend loomed just out of camera view,

eyes redder than a Cannabis Cup judge, jowls quivering with rage.

And holding a fire extinguisher.

"Um—" Paulsen began.

"Prepare to perish, infidels!" The Reverend let loose, filling the studio with a choking cloud of sodium bicarbonate. Paulsen grabbed the end of his tie and held it up to his mouth and nose, which gave his lungs some wiggle room but did little to protect his eyes from the gas. He spun out of his seat, coughing and choking.

Brinkley-Howe screamed and let loose with the pepper spray, the Ambassador pleaded for everyone to calm down and Dr. Sanford whimpered from underneath the table and the aliens, if they were watching, probably fired up the engine of their sweet, cigar-shaped craft in disgust.

Whose idea was it to stop here? Fuck that noise.

"Security[9]!" Paulsen yelled into the cloud of noxious chemicals while his producer wisely pulled the plug on the broadcast and, thusly, our tentative, star-crossed attempt at First Contact.

Sad trombone.

Below the gigantic screen, Alton Grambling and his crew of highly-offended Bible thumpers finally cut

---

[9] Why weren't they already on-scene after the pepper-spray incident? Because this particular failing Fake News Network can't afford anybody but the cable news version of Paul Blart at this point, and it's taken the guy this long to get up the stairs.

through the barrier separating them from its struts, armed with shotguns and a cache of dynamite a local, incredibly pious and incredibly pissed-off miner had helpfully stolen from his job site. Unaware that the broadcast had already ended for all intents and purposes, the Grambling-ites engaged the security forces employed to safeguard the *yuuuge* television, and the amount of shotgunning, eye-gouging and hair-pulling that ensued really put a button on the chemically-fueled brawl relayed on the screen above. When the smoke cleared and the dynamite was rigged to the television's struts, six people were dead and twice as many were injured.

"Clear!" the miner yelled. The Grambling-ites retreated, dragging the remaining injured security personnel to safety because they weren't fucking *monsters*, for god's sake. The miner depressed his plunger, and the dynamite blew the struts apart, and the gigantic (now blank) television toppled over right there in Alton Grambling's cow pasture, destroying the fence he'd spent the previous summer erecting and squishing all those who'd worked so hard to destroy it.

Because they were advanced intelligences, this last event convinced the already-wary aliens to beat feet[10].

The craft rose, disappearing through the clouds and leaving the Earth behind. Its inhabitants were decidedly nonplussed at their terrestrial experience, but they were optimistic sorts, as any species who could keep their shit together long enough to develop faster-than-light travel must be. They decided to see what else our backwater solar system might have to

---

[10] Or equivalent appendages.

offer, and in an inadvertent gesture of solidarity with the humans, they ended up discovering Uranus on a Tuesday[11] themselves.

Which would have given them and the humans something to talk about, if the humans could stop fighting amongst themselves long enough to actually have a fucking conversation.

Pleased by the blessed silence that greeted them, the *spacepeople* spent the next several days exploring the gas giant and its many, many moons (twenty-seven at last count) and, in the end, were far more impressed by the microscopic, methane-based life forms they found beneath Titania's surface than the blathering, gibbering, ultra-violent simian things they'd encountered on the third rock from the sun, and when they finally headed back to their home system to report everything they'd seen they wondered why they didn't just check out Uranus in the first place.

---

[11] Of course, the concept of a "Tuesday" is the sort of anthropocentric fallacy that Brinkley-Howe might violently decry if they read this story, so I would be remiss if I failed to point out that the aliens keyed time to their gestational cycles and spoke using a series of flashes of colored light, so the day on which *they* discovered Uranus was, by their calendar, a three-minute-long burst of mauve. Which isn't terribly efficient. If only our attempts to communicate with them had been successful, we might have been able to trade the Julian calendar for the secret to faster-than-light travel or at least some groovy space rocks.

HEY, NERD!

Are you tired of getting your ass kicked? Are you constantly getting beat up at school, the office, your church?

Well, come on down to Eagle Dragon Martial Arts where we'll teach you how to fly like an eagle AND a dragon! With the combined might of two of nature's deadliest predators, and under the tutelage of ninth-degree karate black belt Skip Baxter, the Most Dangerous Man in Turbo City and inventor of the highly deadly Bax-Do fighting system, you'll be vanquishing your enemies in no time! Bullies? Armed robbers? Stan from accounting? Put a foot up ALL their asses, and more!

I'm Skip Baxter, and I approve this message. Oshirigakusai!

Learn how to Kick Ass the Brian Asman Way™
in

coming Spring 2021!

ACKNOWLEDGEMENTS

There are a couple people I'd like to thank. Myself, of course. Good job, B!

First and foremost, major thanks to John Skipp and Shelly Lyons, who read the first draft and helped me improve it exponentially.

Stephen Graham Jones, Tod Goldberg, and Joshua Malkin, who I'm going to be thanking in most acknowledgements pages.

All my UCR friends who read the first draft of "The Universal Language" and provided invaluable advice.

Max Booth III, for his editing prowess and asking me what the fuck a Spacesquatch smells like.

Lori Michelle for the incredibly easy-on-the-eyes layout you just enjoyed.

Matthew Revert, for the super dope cover.

My agent, Jennie Dunham.

Lucas Mangum and Danger Slater, they know why.

All my horror people, on Twitter and IRL.

You, especially, for reading this book, and if you don't mind maybe give it a review on Amazon and Goodreads?

And Jaclyn, for everything, always.

ABOUT THIS DUDE

Brian Asman is a writer and editor from San Diego, CA. He's the author of *I'm Not Even Supposed to Be Here Today* from Eraserhead Press and has recently published short stories in the anthologies *Breaking Bizarro*, *Welcome to the Splatter Club* and *Lost Films*, and comics in *Tales of Horrorgasm*. An anthology he co-edited with Danger Slater, *Boinking Bizarro*, was recently released by Death's Head Press. He holds an MFA from UCR-Palm Desert. He's represented by Dunham Literary, Inc. Max Booth III is his hype man. Find him on Instagram or Twitter (@thebrianasman), Facebook (brian.asman.14), or his website www.brianasmanbooks.com.

Here's a picture he drew of Ro-Man, the villain of 1953's *Robot Monster*:

(It's an ape in a space helmet)